THE INNOCENT

ALEXANDRA YORK

PROMETHENA PRESS
NEW YORK

PROMETHENA
PRESS

—Bringing fire to the spirit through art—

Copyright © 2015 Alexandra York
WWW.ALEXANDRAYORK.COM

ISBN: 978-0692425145
ISBN-10: 0692425144

This is a work of fiction. Names, characters, places and incidents either are the product of the author's imagination or are used fictitiously, and any resemblance to any actual persons, living or dead, events, or locales is entirely coincidental.

This book was printed in the United States of America

Cover design: SmithMedia
Author Photo: Barrett Randell

PROMETHENA PRESS
New York, N.Y.

This novel is dedicated to all Innocents the world over who suffer not only from evil-doers directly but also from those who will not name evil when they see it

"Non-cooperation with evil is as much a duty as is cooperation with good."

Mahatma Gandhi

Facts: In 2011, 800 FBI and local law enforcement units succeeded in carrying out the biggest single-day crackdown on *La Cosa Nostra* in America's history. 127 people from top *Capos* and *Consiglieri* down to mere Soldiers and Associates were arrested during a sweep so huge that to avoid clogging the courts, the arrested mobsters were processed at an Army base. Although not as publicly visible as thirty-forty years ago, Mafia members are still active in murder, loan sharking, arson, narcotics trafficking, illegal gambling, credit card and business scams, labor racketeering, robbery, prostitute peddling, torture, and extortion. They are also entrenched in certain time-sensitive industries through a process of embedding themselves as second middle-men in delivering perishable products at a higher cost to end users (unsuspecting customers), and they continue to operate on the piers and in numerous national and local labor unions. The Mob in modern-day America may operate in less obvious ways than in past decades—and is largely ignored by the news media now—but especially through infiltration into legitimate businesses it is still deadly and relentless in an underworld of murder and mayhem, destroying not only each other but also many innocent people along the way.

Fiction: The following story, inspired by the facts—

ONE

"LADIES AND GENTLEMEN. ELYSE GANNON!" A small spotlight probed the shadows with a faint but persistent beam until, zeroing in on its target at last, a slender form emerged from the darkness into its path.

The form seemed to glow its way to the tiny platform, and the man wondered why he was disturbed by the image of a setting sun. A sun beautiful but. . .dying.

The man added more champagne to his orange juice, but before he could raise the drink to his lips, he became aware of the low moan of a horn that slipped into the silence unnoticed. Unnoticed, that is, until joined by another equally haunting sound. A sound he now recognized as the voice of a woman.

The form began to move then, all russet and red and gold. The sounds intermingled, the music of a sunset moaning and dying in the dark. The man placed his glass cautiously back down on the table without drinking.

Suddenly, white light flooded the stage, and the woman, in clear view now, threw back her head with a cry—of joy, of life—a cry so untouched by dying that it not only swept aside all images of a sunset but also gripped his chest with inexplicable yearning. The man's eyes narrowed as he watched the woman pursue her song. Her song pursued the man.

He listened intently to her interconnecting chains of melody not noticing that the lines around his mouth had softened into the tenderness of a smile. He concentrated on her varying rhythmic patterns never noticing the rush of youthful eagerness that lifted the normal slouch of his shoulders. He was aware only of her music, clean and pure, hurting him now, touching a hunger he had carried inside for too long, a hunger for sounds such as these, hurting him now while trying to heal him as well.

He expected it because it was mathematically logical, but it came as a shock because it was melodically unique when, one by one, they all began an intricate and complex forging together to make the same statement: first the piano, then the bass, the drum, and finally the horn no longer in its previous flight of counterpoint but staying with her now, and she merging seamlessly with the horn, her voice becoming one of the instruments themselves.

By the time they blended together as one sound—the melody, the rhythm, the words, the instruments, her voice—all reaching the final tonic chord at once, gaily and openheartedly, he felt a burning in his chest, like pain or joy or tension or release, he didn't know which. Both a laugh and a cry, her music grew in him like a forgotten source of hope until bursting through him at last there was no room left for images or memories or wounds, only the calm touch of a promise washing over him like the kiss of a new day.

It was over. The man sat still for a moment. He didn't hear the applause, the shouts for "More, more!" He didn't know he was rising from his seat along with dozens of others.

He knew only one thing: the young woman standing alone on the stage, bowing and laughing, her long copper-colored hair swinging from side to side in happy acceptance, was his enemy. No one had the right to be that good. Not today.

The man laid some bills on the table. Cold resolve lay in his heart. No. He would not meet her now. Would not meet her ever. He would not. Elyse Gannon. He hated her—

TWO

IT HELPED TO DRIVE.

He'd intended to take a commercial flight from Cleveland to New York, but after listening to her sing he felt an uncontrollable need to be in control of something that would respond the way he wanted it to respond. That meant a machine. Programmed properly, his J Boat-J/65 sailing yacht could navigate the ocean via its own complex technology, but he took immense satisfaction in personally commanding its course and altering its tiniest movement by hands-on control. Aside from casual drives along the cliff-hanging beauty of Big Sur, he raced his 12-cylinder Aston Martin DB9 on private tracks just for the jolt of efficacy it afforded. Piloting his twin-engine Piper Seneca V plane with a cruise speed 26% faster than similar models gave him the thrilling flight of freedom and the autonomy of open skies.

On this emotionally turbulent autumn morning he needed the steadying calm derived from wielding control over *any* machine, even a simple rental car, in order to be in close contact with reliable reality, to be touching it, directing it to his will. Machines: Hard. Consistent. There. So much better than people.

His gloved hands were sure on the wheel. Much more sure than they'd ever been on a gun. Without doubt, he preferred the steering wheel of a car in his hands, or the joystick of an airplane, or even the receiver of a telephone.

At age twelve when, like all boys in the neighborhood, he'd been required to learn simple target shooting under his father's patient tutelage, he'd suffered the squirms. Now, thirty-some years later, that same 38-caliber birthday Beretta sat unloaded and unused in a dresser drawer. No. Lorgan Cantrell had never liked guns.

Nor did he like this trip to New York. So a car took longer to get there, giving him additional time to ponder a strategy, if there was one, against the king of strategists. What a mess. When Zio ordered, everyone obeyed. But, Mother of God, this time it just wasn't possible.

The girl was from another time, another place. He shook his head in disgust. That must be why he over-reacted to her. She was born too late. Those days were over and gone. Days of memorable melodies, complex rhythms, and adult lyrics. None of that existed today. Most performers over the last few decades were pathetic freaks, attacking a guitar or a keyboard and shrieking on key or off, it didn't matter which, with a bunch of face-grimacing, bodily disjointed jerks making blasts of loud noise in the background. The rest of the pop singers, although softer in tone, were merely boring, lacking in musical craftsmanship and derivative or repetitive in their lyrics. Rock assaulted the mind and New Age anesthetized it. Rap was not music; it was street rhyme set to a beat. All prevented the faculty of reason from functioning.

Professionalism? Glamour? Even the musically talented ones, the slick ones who perform all over the world to crazed crowds, appeared sexed-up and dressed in costumes as outrageous as their self-branding names. Nothing in the form of real glamour: Class. Beauty. Timelessness. Agelessness. Self-created inner qualities. Qualities not available to the current, shallow flock of musicians nor appreciated by screaming teenagers in giant stadiums. On the opposite end, the small "club spaces" that tried for intimacy failed to match the last few authentic clubs from when he was still very young. One would have to watch old movies to see and hear originality today.

Nightclubs. Where beautifully dressed women and elegant men felt at home in sumptuous surroundings. Where singers were sophisticated artists with individual sounds, some still alive and performing here and there but in their seventies or eighties now. The nightspots currently thriving in big cities were filled with a different breed. Half the audiences wore jeans. Most of the seriously musical cabaret singers substituted external volume for inner emotions and ended up becoming indistinguishable from each other. The solid marriage of secular Rock and religious Gospel they'd heard from babyhood permeated their deliveries of the most romantic songs. Even a world-famous opera diva recently prostituted her spectacular talent to cut an R&B disc, sounding exactly like the rest of the mess. It was all so depressing.

Lorgan pressed his foot farther down on the accelerator. But not *this* girl! How he hated himself for reacting to her this way. Wanting to defend her. Wanting to protect her. Wanting at the same time to kill her career before the rest of the world did. He hated himself, but he hated her more for causing such conflicting feelings in him. The only thing she had in common with today's vocalists was the fact that she wrote her own music. His foot jammed down harder. But what music! Melody, melody, melody. Mother of God! She treated you to it in unending forms, combinations, rhythms, and clean, non-gimmicky vocal deliveries. She obviously had a classically trained voice—he didn't have to be told she graduated from Oberlin to get that—but she whispered nuances to you in her own distinct style of intimate, *popular* music. Only *music* wasn't popular anymore.

How would he mount her career if he were to try it? Talented jazz, Rock, country, and R&B newcomers were easy for him to promote because established musicians in those *genres* acted like welcoming "communities" and always supported his young, up-and-coming singers. But to mount the career of a legitimate adult singer who fit into no category? One who offered not only her distinctive music but her own *person* instead of an artificial "persona"? The problem with this young woman was that she was so damned *individual!* He might be able to guide her into "middle of the road" music, merging opera and pop the way several singers in Italy were doing? Forget it! *She* would never agree to it. Given her independent spirit, it would always be one or the other. She had chosen not classical-pop but pop with class.

He *might* be able to book her into one of the chic New York nightspots that tried to recapture some legitimate past glamour by sticking to Broadway tunes or Great American Songbook standards. But they ended up being copies, singing old tunes. This girl was no copy. He wished he'd never seen her. She had glamour all right, but it was her own style of it. She resonated the best of the past in talent, but she was utterly new at the same time. The future? There was no future in the music business.

The George Washington Bridge appeared suddenly, gleaming in the sunlight, stretching across his vision. He lessened the pressure of his foot, the forecast of a storm settling like rain clouds in his deep blue eyes.

Zio would surely order him to repeat the old Mob pattern of financing a vocalist, paying for coaching, music arrangements, clothes, and placement in the lounge of some Vegas venue or another. But it just wouldn't work with her! It hadn't even worked with all the young hopefuls in the past, because all the Mob could do was give a singer the best chance. The public did the rest. And there was no significant public for this girl today. No *big* market. No *broad* appeal. Knowledgeable aficionados would adore her, worship her, as they did in Cleveland. But where was Cleveland? Without its music-loving audience pool drawn from the nearby college? Nowhere. Most people *anywhere* wouldn't recognize sophisticated music if you danced them to it. They didn't know how to dance either. Even his own generation didn't. There *was* no public expression of inner maturity and physical grace in the culture today—

Today. How he hated it. He was a child of yesterday. Even he was born too late to be a real part of the last-hurrah, creative blowout of his parents' time. And this Elyse? Yesterday, too.

***

"She's yesterday," he said. "It won't work, Zio. I'm sorry," he added respectfully.

It was the first moment the two men were alone since Lorgan arrived. It had been a difficult morning. First, the dreaded entry into New York. He had despised his home city since he was seventeen—the year Doria came to

America. He'd driven up to East 116th Street to put off going to Long Island any sooner than necessary, true, but also to look at the old apartment buildings of his childhood and buy some pork bread. Moreno's was still there, but a huge grocery warehouse had replaced nearly all the row houses of his youth. The neighborhood was unrecognizable. But once the fragrance of hot pork was floating around in his car, he felt a little more comfortable.

How Doria had loved this bread. Freshly eighteen and newly arrived from a small town near the Swiss border to stay with her American aunt and uncle, she was the only northern Italian in his neighborhood. Lorgan had fallen in love with her instantly. Reddish hair instead of black. Blue eyes instead of brown. Fair skin instead of olive. Tall and thin instead of. . . Well, she simply wasn't anything like the other females, young or old, he'd ever seen in his own Italian enclave on the lower fringe of Harlem's east side. Though his own mother was Jewish, her complexion was somewhat dark like so many of the southern Italian women.

Doria was different in *every* way. It didn't matter that she was raised in a convent. She laughed easily. One couldn't imagine Doria on her knees or in a confessional. She was too open, too innocent. It was impossible to conceive of her sinning because if *she* did something amiss, surely God would no longer consider it a sin.

Lorgan had been shy and withdrawn in his youth. He was still withdrawn.

One morning shortly after Doria's arrival, he'd been returning home from Moreno's. You could smell the bread a block away. Doria smelled it. Lorgan was never to forget the way she pulled the paper bag from his arms to bury her face and lose herself in the aroma. Nor was he to forget the sparkling sky-blue eyes that reappeared from the bag beaming with delight at her new-found treasure.

Lorgan heard that young men courted their ladies with flowers or perfume. Doria wanted pork bread. So he brought it to her morning after morning.

Until Rinaldo "Zio" Gadonni came along and took her away from him.

Doria had served the bread this morning—a lifetime later—as if her sense of smell had vanished. Perhaps it was better this way. She was smarter than he. It had been so long. And it was, after all, a youthful infatuation. But it always bothered him that a girl like Doria chose a man like Zio. It wasn't because Zio was old enough to be her father with, in fact, children near her own age from his first wife who had died earlier from cancer. It was just that Zio was so dirty inside, and Doria was so very clean.

Today was the first time Lorgan ever attended one of Zio's famous breakfasts. His father, of course, came whenever he was in town, as did many other men from many other walks of life. Lorgan had heard of the breakfasts, however, begun in the early Mafia heydays when Zio's father was such a power in New York that the mayor of the city was forced to leave a signed, undated resignation with "The Boss" before taking office. That practice died naturally over time as the Mob went more under the radar of public awareness, but even at table today there was a District judge, a prominent real estate developer, an actor and his wife, a couple of Underbosses from Boston, and Zio's eldest son, Reno, who Lorgan understood was now Underboss and his seventy-year-old father's right hand.

Zio had reigned at the head of the table in a silk dressing gown, another old-fashioned habit learned from his famous father, and certain "business" was disposed of over grapefruit. By the time sausage and eggs smothered in marinara "gravy" — and pork bread — arrived, everyone was reaching across one another for second helpings like family or old friends: politicians, businessmen, gangsters — What was that old children's rhyme? "Doctor, lawyer, merchant, thief"?

Rumor spun around that soon after Doria and Zio were married twenty-seven years ago, Zio hired a tutor to teach him the grammar and manners of "better" people. Lorgan's own father, Frankie, said it must be true because Zio's behavior changed so radically after Doria entered his life. But as Lorgan watched Zio clean his teeth with his napkin after breakfast, he had his doubts.

Doria had served them all politely. Her copper-colored hair was still long, he guessed, but it was pulled severely into a knot at the back of her head. Her eyes were still pale blue, but they no longer flashed out at you like sparks in a freshly built fire. Those eyes had been polite, too, at breakfast. As they were now, after the guests departed, gazing at him expressionlessly from a rocking chair in a corner of the living room, while he talked to her husband about their daughter.

"It will work!" Zio's black eyes hardened. He had changed into one of his typical, old-fashioned, conservative, dark blue, hand-tailored suits, white handkerchief peeking up from a breast pocket, waiting to be driven into Manhattan for the day. "Come in." He gestured toward an open doorway at the far end of the room.

"Come in" was a term not to be refused. Lorgan obediently followed the older man into the library, where every wall was lined with books. Doria didn't follow them.

"You see all these books?" Zio demanded. "They are all books I will read before I die. My father read all of them, and I have read most of them already." He swept his arm in an arc over one particular section. "I have read *all* of those."

Lorgan scanned several dozen titles. They all included the name Julius Caesar.

"During Prohibition and the inter-gang fighting it caused," Zio continued, "when my father organized 'our thing'—*La Cosa Nostra*—he studied this great leader and based our military command on his genius. Each of our Families would be commanded by a Boss—I don't use the honorific *Don* anymore, too overused in movies to carry clout in the real world any longer. That's why I use *Zio*, 'uncle,' more friendly. Anyway, under the *Capofamiglia*, the Family Boss, will be a *Sotto capo*, or Underboss, and beneath the Underboss will be *Caporegimi*, lieutenants, who will supervise our squads of Soldiers. Each unit, each Family, will operate under a designated territory. Over all the separate Families in the country, there will be one *Capo di Tutti Capo*, Boss of all Bosses. That is now me! We have *Consiglieri* to advise us legally and help plan strategy. We have a commission, the Ruling Panel, to settle internal disputes peacefully. It doesn't work perfectly, but it's there. So we have *organization*. Without it, forget power. You see?"

Lorgan nodded. Of course he *saw*. This lecture was no more than self stroking from the ego-obsessed Zio because since his own father was Boss of the California Family, it was utterly unnecessary. But why did all this mean—?

"Why does this *organization*, as you say, mean I should marry your daughter?" he asked slowly, hoping the question would not touch off the well-known Gadonni temper. "Especially since I am twenty years her senior? It's one thing to manage her. That I suppose I can try because although outside mainstream music by a long shot, she's very good. But *marry* a woman I don't even know? Why that?"

The temper didn't flare, but Zio looked at Lorgan in exasperation, as if he was proof of what he was about to say. "Because the Members aren't hungry anymore. Because they're not disciplined anymore. Because there's no *respect* anymore. We got three generations American born. The Young Turks are not tough. They play at being gangsters, but they're soft in the guts. They learned how to be Mafia from the movies and TV, not from their fathers, who learned on the streets. *Most of all,* because of that raid a few years ago and the arrest of too many of our top people—the biggest single-day crackdown in American history that even snared your eighty-year-old uncle in New Jersey—the whole organization on the East coast continues to be in sporadic turmoil. And it's not only our own top five New York Families, but like a contagious disease of disorder, it's infecting Families all over the country as underlings feel bolder and dare to vie for higher positions. Mind you, it took 800 of them to bag 127 of us, but they still got so many—*Consiglieri,* Captains, Soldiers and Associates included—they processed the guys at an Army base so as not to clog the courts. This big dent to us was *major,* and even with my own trusted firewall of politicians, I'm lucky to have avoided arrest.

"Plus, because of that one raid's success, the Feds are fanning out now, a little more each year here and there. Plus, Detroit is such an economic-racial toilet, our people are losing control. Plus, Chicago, the gangs. . . You don't keep up with nothing going on, but you do know your own father is hanging on by his fingernails out in Los Angeles because he's called to appear before the Senate from time to time in those damned hearings that pop up whenever some politician needs to get his fat face in front of the public on some juicy subject at election time. Plus! On top of all that shit hitting the fan we all of a sudden got these highly organized Spics from Mexico rumbling heroin into our East Coast territory as easy as they bring in people across the southern border, so they're cutting into our traditional trade big time. Now, I gotta beat the drum with *fresh* organization to deal with all this crap coming at me from all sides.

"So we learn again from history. Later than Caesar. Centuries later, with European monarchies. If we cannot keep discipline and order and strong ties by binding the blood of our fingers with our brothers, we will create them by binding the blood of our children. Giving birth to new children, whose ties because of *inherited* blood cannot be severed."

Zio "The Old Man," as he was called in Mafia lingo, paused and emitted a sigh. "And so, my boy, in this age of space travel and the Internet, we fight a feudal war to maintain power. Most Americans assume *La Cosa Nostra* is a thing of the past. The blockbuster books and movies of thirty-forty years ago are forgotten, and the current films and TV shows are like comic books. So! That raid and the headlines it caused for awhile are again forgotten by the average 'Joe' and 'Jill' out there in Wonderland. Everybody thinks we are now just guys with Italian names in legitimate businesses and our fathers' gangster power is over. They can't imagine we still murder each other, deal in illegal narcotics, loan-sharking, extortion, labor racketeering, robbery, illegal gambling, prostitution, pornography peddling, and all the rest of our sweet-smelling excrement. Ha! Even most union members today are so clueless they don't guess we still control not only the Jersey pier workers but half the other unions they belong to themselves all across the fucking country.

"But *we* on the inside now operate under a wider-lens glare of the Feds and are forced to smooth out our internal skirmishes without causing attention, not even local stuff. Not easy, my boy, not easy. So it's time for me to re-set my position, take charge big-time, put a clear-signal stop to this in-house jumble, and show off my Boss-size cajones by providing new *evidence* that I still maintain control and stability for all members across the country to *see*. Without your father as my usual rock-hard bookend, if I tie the west and east coasts together with a top-level, celebrity-attended bash of a marriage between Princess Elena and you, that event will work just fine to secure me. I hope. . .

"You *will* make Elena a success, and you will do so because otherwise she will never fall in love with you. And she must fall in love with you because she is so stubborn even *I* may not be able to force or blackmail her to marry you if she doesn't love you. She *will* marry you "—the black eyes blackened—"and the sooner the better. Elena is too independent for anybody's good, and she knows more than she knows she knows, if you get my drift. I want her locked into silence by *love*. Blood obviously means nothing to *her*. Plus, if your father doesn't outwit the Senate whenever he's called in and actually gets arrested at some point, I may need to install you early as Boss in California. If my daughter is your wife, I as Elder Statesman can do it. If not," he lifted his manicured hands in disgust."I don't know, the resistance could be too much. You are not well known, and those who do know you think you're a weakling, a Boss's son without even one kill to become a *made member* and taking all that show business stuff seriously— Plus, Plus, Plus! You're half Jewish which is a 'No, No' for a Boss because you're not *all* Italian. But Holy Mary, I have no other choice except *you*—" Zio turned suddenly and stalked out of the room as if he could no longer bear the presence of his future son-in-law, leaving Lorgan to find his own way out. The meeting—the monologue—was terminated.

Lorgan stood helplessly alone in the center of the room. He now understood firsthand how Zio had maintained his absolute power over so many years. Out-strategy him? Defy him? Deny him? Unthinkable. Unthinkable because it was impossible to think at all in his presence. The meticulous formal attire contrasting ridiculously with New York street slang. The well-read vocabulary coming from the mouth of a ruthless thug, who never went beyond the tenth grade. Incongruous. Unpredictable. Unnerving.

But it was the eyes that forbade resistance. Deep not with thought but with experience. Alive not with intelligence but with cunning. Commanding not with conviction but with threats. A killer's eyes.

No one disobeyed Zio. With every fiber of his being Lorgan *wanted* to walk out the door of this house with a "No" flung over his shoulder as the Boss's courageous young daughter had done, but he knew he didn't have the guts to do it. At the otherwise ripe and vibrant age of forty-six he was beyond the time to rebel. It was too late to disobey. Still. . .as he walked slowly to his rental car waiting in the driveway, his mind raced to find an out. By the time he hit the highway to the airport and fly back to Cleveland, he decided he simply would not obey the instructions all the way. He could not go that far and look himself in the mirror. So. Manage Elena Gadonni AKA "Elyse Gannon" he would, which would appease the old man. Seduce her into love and marriage? That he would *not* do. He had worked too hard all his life to stay out of serious Mob "business." This kind of treason against a beautiful, talented, and fiercely independent young woman he would not commit. Managing her career because she was good *not* because she was Zio's daughter would buy him time to figure out how to avoid betraying such a true heroine of the spirit.

THREE

SHE HAD BEEN in her tiny dressing room between sets. He didn't knock on the door or bother with introductions, just walked in and dropped a printed To-Do list, an airplane ticket, a hotel confirmation, and a credit card in her name all clipped together with his business card onto her makeup table. He told her not to be late for any of the appointments on the list, all bills were paid, and he would meet her at the New York dress boutique to select her gowns himself. On his way out of the room, he turned back for one short moment and looked her over as if she was a cow at a country fair. "Lose five pounds before I see you next," he barked. "Publicity photos add weight." Then he vanished as suddenly as he had appeared.

That was just over three weeks ago. She'd laughed delightedly at the closed door, at his nerve, and then dropped the whole package into a waste basket. That's an original big-money "come-on," she thought. But after the show when sharing a fan's gift of champagne, Milo Simms, her always curious horn player, noticed the business card and picked the half-crumpled package from the basket. His excitement finally convinced her to follow the instructions, bizarre as they seemed. Lorgan Cantrell was one of the biggest managers in the business.

By now she knew that his was no "come on." It was all business. He was going to manage her all right. Contracts signed and now in New York for ten days of professional make up lessons, hair style changes, and evening gown selections, she was certain of *that*. But even more than "all business," he seemed very clearly to dislike her, personally, for some unfathomable reason. It wasn't that he did anything overt; it was just his cold, professional eye. A cow at a country fair. He always made her feel like that.

Oh, well, she gave a light skip as she caught her new, glamorized image reflected from a store window, at least he thought the cow could sing. "Moo-oo-oo-oo-oo-oo-oo-oo-oooo," she vocalized up and down the scale as she turned the corner onto a small side street near the border of Harlem's Upper East Side.

She peeked through the small window of his office door in the big, former warehouse building that was now a multi-use rental place. No sign of activity. She knocked, then tried the door. Unlocked. No one was there, but the computer still hummed. The rest was just piles of newspapers, FAX sheets, computer printouts, chewed pencils lying everywhere, and phone numbers written on the walls. She'd found the right place all right. She remembered his apartment in college.

An article headline on his desk caught her eye. "MILLIONS IN SALES TAXES LOST TO MOB CIGARETTE SMUGGLERS." She read on, feeling sick to her stomach.

Interstate bootlegging of cigarettes, a practice that has been growing for decades because of vending machine regulations and astronomically high taxes has reached such proportions that it may be second only to illegal narcotics as a profit item for organized crime.

According to a report by the sub-committee on Inter-governmental Relations, three New York crime Families, including that of Rinaldo "Zio" Gadonni, are suspected of employing more than five-hundred distributors and peddlers in order to smuggle an estimated 480 million packs of cigarettes into New York State alone each year.

In the last ten years, according to Geoffrey Prather, who heads the Council, New York City and State have lost $600 million in tax revenues, the cigarette industry has lost $2.5 billion, half the employees of wholesalers have been thrown out of work, a third of the cigarette wholesalers have gone out of business, and insurance costs have skyrocketed all because of Mob bootlegging and hijacking.

Annoyed, Elyse turned away abruptly and grabbed a pencil. When he walked in, her message was half-written on a wall. Dumping a paper bag with coffee seeping through its sides onto the desk, he scowled at her back. "Who said you could write on my walls Lady?"

She turned around, the sound of his voice happily rekindling deep affection for her best friend. "Hi, Nico."

"Elena Gadonni!" he gasped. And then—the spreading grin telling her she won a beauty contest not a cow show— "No, by God. *Elyse Gannon* for sure now! Jesus Christ, Lady, you changed not only your name but you also have become one *beautiful* Lady!"

The words tumbled out of both of them then. He shared his tuna sandwich and coffee with her, and they fought over the pickle. Nothing had changed. It was as if they had seen each other last week not three years ago at her graduation. Without even her dear mother there, Nico had been the only one to cheer her on.

"All of my gowns are white. One of them cost $5,000. Different styles but every one white. He creates whatever effect or mood he wants with lighting alone."

"My Internet Blog circulation is climbing so fast I may be able to raise subscription charges for my articles very soon. The loyal reader contributions have kept me alive so far, and it's getting better every month."

"He's taking me to California next week. His house is in Malibu by the ocean. We're going to work on arrangements and stuff. His name is Lorgan Cantrell—"

"California? And Cantrell? Frankie Cantrelli? Lorgan Cantrelli maybe?"

"Yes, Nico. 'Lorgan Cantrell.' Everybody's not Italian you know, especially with a first name like 'Lorgan,' silly. Get off it—"

"Sorry." He waved his hand over the desk. "It's a habit— But how did he ever hear of you way out in Cleveland?"

"He knows one of my music Profs at Oberlin. I was a pretty big deal in college, remember?"

"Did you check that out?"

"Nico! He's one of the top managers in the business—"

"Okay, okay. Anyway, I'm going back to American Revolutionary-day journalistic practices. The original newspapers were *action* pamphlets, propaganda sheets, trying to inform and influence readers about *issues*, not fires or rapes, and published for the sole purpose of advocating a cause for freedom. It was a matter of spreading *ideas* then. The reportage and advertising came later. One of the early papers was called *The Prattler*. That's the one I named my Blog after."

"He's letting me keep Milo and the rest of the Cleveland backup. They're coming to California with us for rehearsals. He's booking us first into a small Beverly Hills club for practice and then into a big casino in the Bahamas."

"The Bahamas? A casino?"

"Yup. A *big* casino. It's all so exciting and happening so fast I can hardly believe it."

"The real danger, see, is not the non-objectivity or political agenda of reporters—we all know about that—but in the growing trend by *viewers* to accept media-makers not as competitors in the marketplace of ideas but as 'public utilities' providing the so-called 'truth.' Then not understanding the inherent temptation to *make* news instead of *report* it, they fail to critically examine the information they receive with the skepticism required."

"The guys and I feel this could be our real chance—"

"Are you going to see your family while you're in town?"

"Of course not. You know I haven't seen them in years.

"Not even your mother?"

"No."

The conversation halted awkwardly as Elyse and Nico stared at each other for a long, remembering moment.

"I see you're still doing investigations like that." She pointed to the cigarette article.

"Yeah, sure. You know, I didn't grow up on the sheltered North Shore of Long Island like you did. Half my high school class from 116th Street is solidly in the Mob now, so my sources get better all the time. Besides, I do have a very longstanding *personal* score to settle. . ." Nico paused. "But

I don't go around surprising little girls by telling them their very own family is a *La Cosa Nostra* Family with their father the actual top Boss."

Elyse felt a thud in her gut. It still hurt. "That's nice of you," she said dully.

"Did you know your brother Paulie—the only other college educated member of your family besides you— is deep into Mexican-delivered drugs now? *Paulie the Professor* in Mob lingo? *The Old Man* doesn't know where he's getting the stuff, just glad Paulie's keeping it in the Family 'cause so much of it is bypassing the Mob now."

"My half-brother."

"He started setting up a few underground bars in middle-class sections of Boston and Hartford a few years ago. The 'guests' can order whatever *fix* they want, just like the old Prohibition-day alcohol drinks, but now he's expanded into the chic, international trust-fund baby hangouts because cocaine and especially heroin have really become, pardon-the-pun, *mainstream*. He has a new bar behind a Greek restaurant right here on the east side, And how about your sister? I'm sure you don't know the latest. I just got the poop myself—"

"My half-sister."

"Well, Claretta's new handle is 'Dumdum'. It's because she's using a bullet called 'dumdum' for her hit jobs now. They flatten on impact and cause big, gaping, jagged holes in their victims before they die. They're hollow-point bullets she claims are just as effective as the conventional kind but reduce the dangers of secondary hits to innocent bystanders because they tend to remain in the victim's body rather than passing through. How about that?"

"Nico, please! I don't want to hear all this—"

"Okay. But you should see your mother. She never knew about your father's 'business' either."

FOUR

2:00 A.M. DORIA LOOKED without curiosity at the clock as she sat curled up in her robe in a wicker porch chair next to her husband, watching the rented movie on TV. Since Elena left home for college in Ohio eight years ago, she and Rinaldo had lived alone in their sixteen-room house. They had four color TVs in other places, but her husband always insisted they watch the old black and white portable in the basement's spare bedroom late at night. It never really mattered, she supposed, since all he ever wanted to see were old cowboy movies, and half the time they were in black and white anyway. After a year or two of dragging the wicker chairs in from the porch in summer or the garage in other seasons each evening when they returned from restaurants with friends or family dinners—and their family was *large*—she just left them in the basement bedroom permanently. His chair had a yellow pillow on it. Her pillow was red. They never took each other's chairs.

For all those years, she just assumed it was a funny little quirk on the part of her husband to watch TV in the basement at the end of an evening out, but since that day five years ago when Elena charged into the house with all her questions, Doria realized that the location was chosen for safety. No windows. No outside doors.

She never noticed before that day, either, that their home on Frances Avenue was any different than any other on the neat, quiet, upscale suburban street in Sands Cove. The shrubbery was trimmed a little lower than the neighbors, true, and at night the lighting outside was brighter, but those were not necessarily suspicious things. She knew about the extensive burglary system, the one-way mirror at the front door, and the photoelectric eye installed in all the windows that would sound an alarm if anyone tried to open them from the outside, but this was Long Island, after all, and crime was spreading from Queens and Brooklyn every year, especially with all the illegal aliens invading the country. In the past, she felt warmed by the fact that her husband was so overprotective of her and Elena's safety.

There had always been rifles among the paraphernalia in the basement, but Rinaldo explained he used to be a deer hunter, so even those didn't seem unusual. There had also been a rifle behind the curtains in their bedroom as well, but once again, it was explained to her as a normal precaution against a world filled with crime. There were a few pistols, too, in drawers here and there, but these were perilous times. Everyone took extra precautions. They even had friends in rural Buck's County, Pennsylvania, where the local police put up signs that the area was patrolled by civilian "deputies" because there was a rash of robbers breaking into uninhabited homes during the day when everyone was at work or school and ransacking homes of anything valuable. Then there were the new gun control laws, and some people worried about government oppression here in America of all places and wanted their own firearms at hand. So they said on TV anyway.

The rifle behind the bureau in the guest room she hadn't known about until Elena found it when she was three years old. Her daughter had pulled it out from its hiding place and, playing with the trigger, blasted a hole through the ceiling into the second-floor den where Rinaldo was napping. He and his ever-present men friends came running and yelling from all over the house only to find little Elena sitting on the rug in her pajamas, whimpering with fright, the smoking rifle at her side. After that incident, all guns disappeared from the interior of the house. Or at least Doria thought they did.

She knew about the one, ever-present pistol with the intricately wood-inlaid handle on top of her husband's bureau in their bedroom, but he explained it was an antique given to him by his immigrant grandfather, so he kept it as a decorative memento of old Italy. He kept tubes of dimes and quarters on top of that bureau, too, saying he didn't want a cell phone because of some radiation danger to the ears that she didn't understand, but he knew where there were still pay phone booths here and there in case he needed to make a call from outside the house. She also knew he kept private business papers in the always-locked top drawer, but since so many of his friends and business associates were always around and able, she supposed, to snoop in their bedroom when they were both away for one reason or another, this made sense to her, so she never pried. That bureau was "off limits" to everyone except Rinaldo. Doria always placed freshly laundered shirts, undershorts and socks at the foot of the bed for him to put away himself, and if Elena had ever been a bad girl as a child, he would take her favorite toy and put it on top of the bureau as punishment. The child knew she could touch nothing there, even when she was older and could reach for it.

The storage room in the basement was always lined by shelves packed with canned goods, boxes of pasta, jars of store-bought tomato sauce, tins of coffee, and bottles of wine, soft drinks, juices, and mineral water—there was always enough food and drink there to make it unnecessary to shop for months—but she never found that surprising because Rinaldo's men friends were constantly in the house, cooking up all sorts of different things, so they would need a pantry stocked with a variety of goods. Most Italian men hung around together and loved to cook. She never minded. It took the kitchen load off her.

She looked over at her husband of twenty-seven years. She had been so young and insulated from the world by her convent upbringing that, to her, this man was suave, sophisticated, handsome, and a dream come true when he asked for her. Now, he was snoring like an old man. She had never yet known him to stay awake to see the conclusion of a movie, but he would never let either of them go to bed until it was over.

Rinaldo was seventy now, but he still had all his own teeth, and his head was still full of jet-black hair. There wasn't an ounce of fat anywhere on his body, and he ate a plate of spaghetti every day of his life. He'd always been a strict but affectionate father to Elena, a good husband to her, attentive and generous except for his temper, but even those unpredictable outbursts were short-lived. He was an excellent cook and a good singer, too. He wasn't trained formally, of course, but very forceful when he sang along with their opera recordings. He went to Mass every Sunday and gave large amounts of money not only to the Church but to many other charities as well. He was an admired and wealthy but generous businessman, always giving no-interest loans to elderly people and old friends back in the Bronx, and he had among his friends a former mayor, current judges, CEOs of big companies and many small businessmen from all over the country, as well as a bevy of bright and shiny socialites and entertainers.

How could she ever have guessed he was not only a criminal—and a killer—but the head of the entire Italian organized crime syndicate in America?

She had not believed it when twenty-year-old Elena came storming into their home and accused her father of those things. And when he threw their only child out of the house in indignation, Doria sided with her husband. But then Claretta, Rinaldo's forty-five-year-old daughter from his first marriage, confirmed Elena's accusations as true. Because she was proud of the truth. Because she was part of it. Because she became the first female *made member* in the whole *Cosa Nostra* many years ago while still in her early twenties.

After the confrontation with Elena, Rinaldo talked to his men in front of Doria as if she didn't exist. Later, when Elena sent Doria copies of old newspaper clippings given to her by a collage classmate, she waited until her husband was in Manhattan for the day and took out their wedding album just out of curiosity. After looking through photos of guests pictured at tables and on the dance floor and matching some of the faces with those in the publications, she watched the professionally filmed wedding video that was stored in the library along with now-antiquated cowboy cassettes and identified even more. They were all there. America's biggest Mafia criminals along with Hollywood stars and prominent politicians. In the past, she and Rinaldo had looked at their wedding video many times for pleasure together, and he always made love to her afterward with special ardor.

Since Elena's outburst and banishment, she had resigned herself to her own position by continuing to submit to her husband's physical desires whenever he wished, but since the revelation of who he really was, she felt nothing for him. She was only grateful that God had not given her more children by this man.

Her weeping aroused her husband. "Why are you crying?" he asked. "A sad cowboy movie?"

Doria sobbed. "Please leave her and her career alone, Rinaldo. She hates us. You disowned her. Can you not let her live in peace?"

Rinaldo Gadonni's black eyes leapt from sleep. "Do not ever talk to me about Elena again, woman. You who lie like a corpse in bed now—"

But Doria continued, pleading with him. "She's in New York, Rinaldo. Maria Tatalo saw her on Madison Avenue with Lorgan. May I please see her? Please Rinaldo? She's my only child!"

"And she is the only child of *mine* who does not show me *respect*" he shouted back, the famous temper rising fast. "But she will *learn* to show me respect once she marries that weakling Lorgan Cantrelli, and especially after she has her first baby. You will show me respect, too, and never speak to me of her until she *is* married and becomes part of our Family again because then she will *also* be part of the California Family. I *need* California, and if Frankie gets indicted or can't make a deal with the Feds, Lorgan is the only one to take over out there. I need Elena to be his wife— the daughter of the *Tutti Capo* of the whole country—me!— in order to hold this thing together by controlling both coasts until we all get fully back under the radar and forgotten by *everyone*, including those dickheads in Washington."

Doria watched through tears as her husband, the dashing man she once revered as a knight in shining armor, turned off the TV and raged upstairs to bed. She stood slowly, dabbed her eyes with a tissue, and followed him. They had never had such an open conversation in their entire lives together. He seemed obsessed with California and bringing *her* precious daughter back into *his* Family. She had hoped he would at least let her see Elena now that Lorgan was representing her, but he just made it clear that she could not.

So now she needed to *think* for the first time in her gilded-cage existence. *Think for herself.* She couldn't defy her husband directly, but as a mother she couldn't let this travesty take place without doing something to protect her only child. How and when she didn't know, but she must become mentally prepared to think and to act against her husband. She felt weak and strong at the same time.

FIVE

LORGAN CANTRELL wasn't a large man, but he was in superb physical shape. Elyse watched him from her guest bedroom window as he sat by the swimming pool sipping his morning orange juice, his two beautiful Alaskan Huskies lying asleep at his feet.

Even though it was Sunday, the splashing of water had awakened her as usual. Lorgan rose at 6:30 every day of the week and lapped a full mile in his Olympic-size pool, rain or shine, before reading the newspaper and checking his e-mail over a large glass of juice. She never knew anyone to drink so much orange juice, straight or laced. In the evening he mixed it in reverse proportions from the normal brunch-time Mimosa—more champagne than juice—making the drink festive, light and tangy. She had grown to like it this way as a before-dinner cocktail herself.

Elyse guessed her manager to be in his mid-forties, but his black hair contained no gray. It was the way he styled it, she guessed, brushed fully back from his face with no part, giving his appearance a young, windswept look. His face, though, was always absent of any expression. If he ever felt anything at all, which she doubted, he kept it buried deep in his dark blue eyes, eyes the color of the sea at dusk, still clear but very dark. He was wearing white bathing trunks slit on both sides just enough to draw attention to his muscular thighs.

After spending a month in his contemporary home that hung dramatically out from a cliff over the ocean in Malibu, she was certain he owned no other color. White belonged to him. White marble, white carpeting, white draperies, white furniture, white everything. Even his dogs were white. White and light. Clear glass floor-to-ceiling windows supported by white stone pillars formed the spacious shape of his house, featuring the sky above and the water below. White and light. That was Lorgan.

Elyse wrapped a short, white, kimono-style silk robe around her nude body and slipped into the exquisite gold-mesh, high-heeled slippers that Lorgan suggested to show off her slim, shapely legs.

Stepping carefully down clear Lucite stairs, she headed to the kitchen for some orange juice of her own. Even private clothing that few if anyone would ever see, he lectured her, would show in her performance, because what you choose to wear in private reflects who you really are on the inside and affects your outward demeanor at all times. The staircase seemed to float between the two floors, and at night each individual stair was softly illuminated from somewhere within its interior. Milo and the other guys hated the place because it seemed a fragile house, but she loved every dramatic bit of it.

The thing she loved most was the Lucite Baby Grand with a mirrored top. Lorgan decided she would open her act in a Beverly Hills club sitting on top of it, an old-fashioned idea for cabaret singers but fresh and new because of the Lucite. In other, far-away clubs the pianos would be standard black, but she carried the lightness and the elegance of Lorgan's piano inside her now. She would always sing as if she were perched on *his* piano for her opening song. Bringing her juice to the living room, she stepped up to the tiny, white marble stage and, leaning over the piano, toyed with a new composition. Sunday was such a lovely, relaxing day here.

Unlike the rest of the week. She now knew what it must feel like to be an athlete in training. Six days a week she was required to swim with her manager. Not a full mile, perhaps, but a full half-hour. He refined her stroke until it was strong and smooth and graceful. It would show up later in her walk, he said. Then, after a breakfast of grapefruit, cottage cheese, and a boiled egg—he still wanted her weight down—she took a dance lesson in the cabana by the pool with an elderly instructor who had once been a well-known ballroom dancer. Lorgan didn't mind that she never studied ballet, but he wanted her to learn the waltz, the rumba, the tango. She wasn't awkward, but he wanted more fluidity in her physical bearing because, he insisted, the entire body must understand music.

The pool cabana housed another of her favorites. A 1946 Wurlitzer jukebox contained old big-band records, providing music for her dance lessons. Tubes of quarters lying on top of it originally sent a cold shiver through her— Zio's bureau—but then she learned they were for the antique machine. One quarter for five songs. A nickel for each glorious sound!

She walked lazily out to the cabana now and, inserting a quarter, pressed some buttons. As the romantic music flowed out into the room, little bubbles began to flow inside the yellow plastic tubes that encircled the edges of the huge, wood-encased machine, and a blinking red star in the center winked on and off as if a reminder of just plain good-natured fun. All this was from another time and another place, but even though she was well aware of the big band era and The Great American Song Book tunes, she'd still learned a great deal from becoming more closely connected to them here in this intimate setting. Her college degree proved her mastery of the mathematical aspects of music, and she knew her own compositions carried a distinction of their own. But her time here with Lorgan was teaching her much more about the subtleties of style and the minute details that lead to perfection of performing. Milo with his sexy trumpet and her backup combo players of piano, bass, and drums were advancing their skills, too. After her dance class each morning, she rehearsed alone with them until lunch, and she could already hear the sophisticated changes.

It was after lunch, however, that work really began for all of them. Lorgan drilled them mercilessly. Refining. Honing down. Getting rid of the extraneous and going after the purity of a phrase, a harmony, even the length and coloration of a single note. He was relentless. They already knew the music, he told them. Now he wanted their individuality, their essence, their souls. And the nuances he was after *were* beginning to surface with consistency. She could hear it. She could feel it. Their sounds were much cleaner, more disciplined, and by becoming more intensely purposeful, they sounded more relaxed and natural. As he said they would. Endless practice. Little things. Nothing escaped his attention.

During the past week they began to work with lighting, and she rehearsed in an evening gown. The guys were forced to wear jackets—no ties but no jeans either. Lorgan taught the group how to utilize the Key spotlight for their solos, and he taught her how to sing the sensuousness of silk. It had been during the past week, too, that she glimpsed for the first time a small spark appearing occasionally in his deep blue eyes. At certain moments in the evening after standing back in the darkened room to watch while they rehearsed on stage bathed in ever-changing color showers of light, he would walk over to comment or criticize. It was then and only then that she caught a glimmer of pleasure in his eyes. At those times, she felt an uneasy, inner stirring. That glimmer in his eyes seemed to originate from somewhere deep within him, but it also seemed to pull her toward it in some fascinating way on a thrilling but dangerous journey in search of its source.

She walked out of the cabana and, wandering to the edge of the patio, looked nearly a hundred feet straight down past a smooth wall of red rock into a peaceful Pacific Ocean. Lorgan's eyes were the color of the Atlantic, she decided.

The poolside patio was surrounded by a low, white marble parapet no more than two-feet high. Gardenia bushes formed a flower guard around it on the ocean side, edging the expansive view with their delicate white petals and fragrant perfume. She reached for a blossom and held it to her nose. She would always carry one when she sang, she decided, reminiscent of the signature flower Billy Holiday always wore in her hair. She smiled. Lorgan couldn't object. Gardenias were white—

It was exhilarating to stand unobstructed like this at the patio's precarious edge, but it was also obvious that no children visited this house. She could see Lorgan's sleek sailboat moored to a buoy far away from the rocky shore and looking like a spectacular white speck in the water below. They had not been invited even to board it for a look-see let alone sail it during their stay. Everything with Lorgan was work. She stepped up onto the parapet and stared out at the boat with curiosity. Did he sail it alone?

"You little fool!"

She cried out with fright as his arms, firm and urgent around her waist, lifted her off the marble stanchion and dragged her roughly back to the solid patio floor, both dogs growling nervously but standing at bay.

"I don't allow children here at all, but I might have thought any adult would have some sense. I've invested far too much time and money in you by now to have you waste it all by falling over the edge. There are nothing but rocks down there. You fool!"

Elyse looked up into his eyes. He was still holding her tightly, bending her painfully backward over his arm as he shouted at her. His breath was warm, smelling faintly of oranges and gardenias. The muscles of his face pulled back in anger starkly accentuated the high cheekbones and the square jaw. His eyes were unguarded now, the bottom of their bottomless depths momentarily visible, revealing the source of the spark she had only glimpsed before: *the source of his personal passions. . .* for music, for sailing, for white, for. . .?

She leaned back farther in his arms, staring into his eyes with open wonder, knowing she was seeing the real Lorgan Cantrell for the first time.

SIX

WHAT WAS HE doing it all for? He knew why. Out of respect for her stunning talent and supreme independence combined with his own life-long hatred of the Mob, it was worthwhile to *really* train her, groom her, and encourage her and the combo to rise to their best. It was a long shot— maybe just wishful thinking?—but if he could establish her career solidly enough to find a small but loyal audience that could rocket her name to *some* celebrity status fast enough, she might truly escape all traps her father would surely set for her return to The Family. Like dissidents in totalitarian countries, if their names become famous enough, the powers that be are likely to leave them alone for fear of public outrage more dangerous than the ranting dissident. If he were able to do this one honorable thing for this one honorable woman, it might absolve him of all the sub-talent wannabes he'd taken on under pressure from one Mob Boss or another whose careers had gone nowhere but had made him independently wealthy and kept him outside the fray of serious Mafia dealings.

Zio's daughter was so good she *should* be championed *without* any insider help, but this he could not avoid. He had to use Mob connections to get her started. And she would never know. She was too young and ambitious to suspect him, and his name was too well established. The problem was that no matter how he tried to remain aloof from her personally, she *was* beginning to become curious about him as a man. He could see it in her eyes, and he hated her for finding any interest between them except music. It was too close to Zio's plan and too far from his own. But most of all, he hated himself for his reluctant but unavoidable duplicity in this treachery of Zio's, so for his own sanity and both their sakes, he must save Elyse and, in fact, himself from the ultimate end game of—Mother of God—*marriage*.

All Zio wanted was to solidify the California-New York bond, so the rest of the Bosses who weren't already in jail would continue to bow to him as *Tutti di Capo*, and he would be able to hang on to his supreme power. That damned raid a few years ago had splintered many of the Families. Several mid-level Captains had ratted on others to save their own asses and the lines of authority were becoming disrupted in a few strategic places beyond New York. If his father survived the periodic Hearings without squealing or getting indicted, Lorgan wouldn't have to worry about taking over his own Family for many years. His father was sixty-eight and in good health. But Lorgan didn't *want* to take over. *Ever!* And he didn't want Elyse to love him. *Ever!*

He looked over at her now in the seat next to him, wrapped up to her chin in a blanket and sleeping soundly like a little girl. Milo and the other members of the combo were back in the Coach section of the plane. They had all worked so hard. Mother of God—!

What had he done in his life to bring him to this? A day when he would take an innocent twenty-five-year-old woman and fake the path that might make her a star? When he'd taken on other singers for a Mob member now and then, he'd at least let their careers forge their own alleyway. He managed them, yes, but he never used Mob connections to make something happen that wasn't natural. Now, nothing he was doing was natural.

How could he ever lead a Mafia Family? Even though he was the eldest son, taking his father's place had never really crossed his mind as a concrete fact. He'd spent his whole life *trying* to stay clean and as far away as possible from the grime. He was no leader of anything, and Zio knew that. His brother Carmine was much better suited for the role, but he was a year younger and already married with other duties of his own.

It was pointless to keep revisiting the event, but none of this would have become necessary except for that damned raid. For several decades, *La Cosa Nostra* had operated with very little public awareness. Made members had backyard barbeques with their unsuspecting neighbors all over the country and carted their kids to school and soccer games just like everybody else in the legit world. But now, with the Feds still poking around here and there and Frankie in an uncertain position, Zio actually *did* need a stronger liaison to California. With Philly and Detroit drowning in their own muck, Los Angeles was the only Family in the country second in power to his own. Elyse was the one available child left. Although some Underbosses had been arrested, Zio's other daughter, "Dumdum" Claretta, was still running operations in Boston with her husband, his youngest son Paulie was moving his drug business to Chicago, his eldest son Reno would take over New York,

Lorgan's Uncle Tony headed up Florida, so Zio was secure in those places.

But Texas, Arizona, and New Mexico were still unsettled. With—think of it!—a couple of *Capos* and even one actual Boss already in jail, their internal hierarchy was vulnerable to internal unraveling at the seams. So Zio *did* need to re-establish his hold on the western territories by securing California. Okay. Lorgan could understand the Boss's thought processes: The strongest Families in the country headed by Zio's Family members to keep the rest of the others in tow. It was a logical plan, but Lorgan just *couldn't* become an active part of such a rotten endeavor, let alone drag Zio's fiesty and innocent daughter along with him.

Furthermore, "Elyse" wasn't *Elena* anymore. She really had become her new, chosen name on the inside and, now with his help, publicly as well. What had he ever done to deserve advancing this horrific sham? He felt sick to his stomach—

Nothing. Precisely the answer of course. He had not wanted to soil his own soul, so he managed to avoid becoming a *made member*—He never killed anyone. But he dined with many men who *did* kill. At age eighteen and under order from his father he also had taken "Omerta," the oath of silence. He hadn't wanted to do that one act of commission rather than his ordinary habit of omission, but his father was Boss; there was no choice. He also took payoffs to represent his father's Hollywood friends in the entertainment world and, in fact, would not be the important agent-manager he was today without super-name singers like Darien King and Cally Creston in his stable.

Yes, he kept himself alone and away from the filthiest

gang in the country, away from the drugs, the fraud, the blood. He stayed in his pure, white, unstained house in the hills. No *Cosa Nostra* member ever set foot in it, not even his own immediate family. The one exception was his cousin Jason from the Jewish side, who sailed *Dreamer* with him. But even though he and Jason weren't active in the Families, they both *knew*. Somewhere along the way they had silently condoned it all by remaining on the fringes of such an organization and taking the crumbs without ever acknowledging who baked the cake.

All this never bothered him before because he never allowed himself to think about it before. He gazed at the peacefully sleeping figure beside him. And he had never, personally, cheated anyone either.

Zio wouldn't agree to letting Elyse open in Beverly Hills as Lorgan planned. Her father needed more control than giving her a debut gig in *Lorgan's* show business territory. So Zio insisted that she open at the Bahamas casino because Carmine ran the gambling junkets there, and he would absolutely *assure* her success. Elyse would never know because she would be enchanted with her new, white-sequined evening gown, the casual but smart tuxedo-type jackets on her backup guys, the haute cuisine and the fine wines, the glittering ocean, the cloudless sky, and her own exciting and successful debut.

She wouldn't know that the women handling the Twenty-One games had marked cards or that the switchmen who moved the mercury-loaded dice in and out of the games controlled the numbers. She wouldn't dream that card and dice games were only part of the action upstairs in the hotel, the other part being made up by Broads who "entertained" visiting Suckers with drugs in their drinks and hot sex in another room, followed by

"Cool-off" men who, after a Sucker realized he'd been stripped of his money by a Broad, would calm the Sucker down and make him feel he'd had a good run for his money. And if the Sucker didn't cool down, more Broads — two or three *classy* hookers this time — would take him into another room and collectively take his mind off his losses with group sex so kinky and mind-bending that he was too delirious to care about his losses. And if that *still* didn't work, videos of the Sucker and the Broads to be delivered to his wife *always* cooled him down. Lorgan's Uncle Tony from Miami actually owned the casino. Carmine supplied the Suckers from all over the world. The Arabs, in particular, were easy marks because they had so much money to lose, and booze and Broads were against their religion, so the videos cooled them down real fast.

No. Elyse wouldn't know about any of this. The problem was that *he* knew. He may never have taken part of any of it directly, but he always knew. The plane they were on right now carried a party of thirty Suckers going to the same casino where Elyse would sing. Carmine never chartered private planes but worked out special excursion deals with commercial airlines. For every fifteen passengers, he got one ticket free. For every thirty people, two tickets, and so on. The head of this particular junket was working the aisle right now, mingling with the gambling people to determine which ones to set up. Carmine also ran junkets to London, Moscow, and Monte Carlo. The whole operation was a gold mine. All the Mob had to do was dig.

The Suckers would blame themselves, of course. No one twisted their arms to gamble or join the upstairs orgies. But even though Lorgan never wanted to be a part of it, he was born to be part of it. It was like being born into royalty. You either continued in your designated place, or you were thrown out, or you were rubbed out. *Nobody* left on their own.

Well, all right, there it was. *That's* why he disliked this girl so intensely. She had done it. When she found out about her Family, she repudiated them, proving it *could* be done. Even if she was roped back into it by one of her father's schemes, she would still be untainted because she would have been duped. She would never act voluntarily to participate in any activity that promoted *La Cosa Nostra's* evil.

Plus she was so very good a singer. Again, he reminded himself that *this* was why he was grooming her seriously. Not that her chances were great. She probably wouldn't ever make it big in today's impoverished music world, but if it *could* be done as he fervently hoped it might, elevating and refining her already-considerable abilities is the way he would do it. In a very real sense, the girl was everything he had ever secretly valued. She was independent, where he was a reluctant parasite. Talented, where he had foregone his own music ambitions to take the easy way out and promote others. Courageous, where he remained too weak to fully jettison the security provided by his background.

The only possessions he truly valued in his life were his home, his two blue-eyed dogs that were his constant companions, his art collection that spanned two centuries, his sailboat that gave him freedom of the open sea, and his Aston Martin that was like driving a jet on the ground. His twin engine plane he used infrequently, but when he did go to the small airport where it lived and lift off the ground for a sky-cruise practice session, he also felt lifted above all the dirt below. For some reason, he could feel an inner sense of his himself with his treasures, feel some sense of the real Self as he might have been. No! He would *not* possess this woman no matter what, because if he did she would be an ever-present reminder of who he might have been but never was.

Elyse awoke refreshed and feeling light. She smiled over at Lorgan, into eyes that were staring at her intently. The eyes were filled with resentment. The spark was gone. She frowned. What could she possibly have done to elicit such hostility from him? She turned away quickly before he could see tears beginning to gather in her own eyes.

SEVEN

LOU ROSHARD SLAPPED a hundred-dollar tip into the Cool-off man's hand. "Hey, man, don't sweat it. It was worth the grand I lost just to see those two Congressmen screwing the same chick. Never seen Democrats and Republicans getting along so well. "Hey, man, see ya, right?"

The Cool-off man laughed. "Sure *man*, see ya." He shoved Roshard roughly out the door.

Lou swayed only slightly on his way to the elevator. He wasn't drunk—he hadn't given up gambling, but at least he'd given up boozing—he just felt light-headed with relief to be away from that crowd. He really didn't mind losing the money since he now had plenty. It was the whole bizarre upstairs scene that unnerved him. Well, what the hell, he stepped into the casino, maybe it *was* worth it to see those two Congressmen go at it together on one broad.

The "regular" games were in full swing now. Dinner and the main show over, people were back to drop another bundle of money. Some folks, especially Americans, seemed never to leave the Slots at all, not even to eat. He'd seen more than one fat-assed female eat a sandwich, drink a beer, insert quarters or bills, and push buttons all at the same time without ever breaking her rhythm.

But upstairs was where the action was. Never knew about that kind of thing before except, maybe, in movies. Now he knew more about a whole lot of real-life things than he wanted to know. Funny. Everybody thinks if you live in New York you know everything. Not so. The Bahamas was a world unto its own.

Oh yeah, he was learning a lot of new things lately. He'd just met a Senator, two judges, some big businessmen, some small businessmen, and a few movie actors. Where else could he meet that outwardly diverse group except at such a phenomenon as an upstairs card game? And everyone seemed to be there for the same reason: to rub shoulders with everybody else. Politicians wanted the glamour of Hollywood, and movie stars wanted to bask in the power of politicians. Big businessmen wanted favors from the politicians, and small businessmen wanted to pretend they were *big* businessmen. And the Mob wanted the money and sanction of all. Now *that* was mutual admiration. Plus, everybody wanted a little naughty fun together, as if getting away with something forbidden in collective form made it okay. God-a-mighty, he might be learning the hard way, but he certainly was getting an education these days. He looked nervously at his hands, remembering Reno's threat. Well, no choice about it. Might as well get it over with.

The small bar-lounge just off the main gambling room was noisy and hopping with people willing to pay for drinks. He slouched into a booth. "Milk," he shouted to the waitress as she sailed by his table to deliver drinks to a neighboring table. "In a big glass—"

He looked up toward the small stage. That must be the group playing now. He couldn't hear them because of the loud chatter around the place, but he observed the unusual set-up. Clever gimmick: A white girl with an all black backup group. Nope, the drummer was white. He still couldn't hear, but the girl, the way she moved in that graceful but stylized way— Choreographed for sure but outwardly perfectly natural. Maybe he wouldn't have to fake it after all.

Leaning over to the table next to him of about eight people, he whispered, "Hey, listen to this girl for just one song, she's real special. Hey, pass it on—"

The folks at the table laughed at the game, and each person turned to someone else at another neighboring table. "Hey, listen to this girl for just one song. She's real special. Pass it on"

Lorgan looked up suspiciously from his corner table near the stage. The audience was suddenly, inexplicably quiet. Everyone was sitting expectantly, waiting for the next number. He frowned. *What. . .?*

Elyse laughed into the microphone. "Well, Hello!" she greeted the crowd. Then to her guys, "Heroes."

Lou hunched over the table and tore a napkin into small pieces while he listened. He didn't look at the group now, just let their music hit him any way it wanted to. He always judged a new group this way.

Elyse was suddenly back in Lorgan's living room, leaning into the Lucite piano and singing out to one man standing at the back of the darkened room. It was the first attentive audience they'd garnered all week. She hadn't minded. Neither had the guys. They were flying high together on their first big trip. This was only the beginning.

47

But word must have gotten around sooner than expected. She beamed exultantly at the man in the dark and sang for him alone.

Then she heard it.

The applause.

And then silence again. They were listening!

Lou looked around him with new interest. The game was over, but the girl had them on her own terms now. Hey! He smiled a slow smile.

Lorgan tilted back in his chair, eyes narrowed, watching the audience. He didn't need to watch Elyse. He knew every lift of her finger. But the audience was with her. Not everybody. Many had gone back to their conversations, but politely now. And others were really with her. Mother of God—

Elyse threw her gardenia happily into the crowd and began to leave the stage, but a hand grabbed her arm.

"Hey, Baby! You are dynamite. Bring your backup and have a drink with me."

Lorgan placed a hand firmly on Lou's shoulder. "If you have anything to say to the lady, you can speak to me."

"Oh, sure," Lou grinned amicably. "You her manager? Hey, man, I'm on the level. Here's my card."

They all sat down at a big, round table, and Lou ordered milk for everyone. "Only trouble is, man, *you* gotta go," he said, pointing at Bobby.

The drummer laughed. Lou's affability was contagious, and the fact that they were all sitting around drinking milk was so zany— "Why man? You don't like my skins?"

"No, that ain't it. I don't like your *skin*. Too white, man. You draw attention away from the chick. Her backup gotta be *all* black."

"I'd like you to meet my backup, Sir," Elyse cut in firmly.

"Milo Simms, trumpet. Bill Jackson, piano. Louis Haynes, bass. *And* Bobby Jones, drums."

Lou studied her thoughtfully, another slow smile lifting the corners of his mouth. "O—kay, Baby." He turned to Lorgan. "She's right. This chick got no need for gimmicks. Audience out there for her, man. Same one watches old movies on TV and won't go to new trash-action stuff. Same one keeps American Songbook singers eating good. Same one wants novels with plots and art that can hang only one way. That's her audience, man. And it's *there,* if anyone would take time to notice. I got so much crap I'm cutting every month. Let me cut a disc with this kid, just for the fun of it, just because she's *good.* All her own songs and couple of oldies just for luck."

Lorgan took the card offered him. "How old are you?" he asked Lou.

"Twenty-three, man. But I know good stuff when I hear it, and I even mix bad stuff good. I like that sound of hers. Class, man."

EIGHT

ASTONISHED, ELYSE PEERED over at the clock. 6:30 AM. Then she picked up the phone still half asleep.

"Get dressed and pack. I'll meet you in the lobby in a half-hour."

Astonishment turned to full-awake anger. She spat the words into the mouthpiece. "And *you*, Mr. Manager, *Sir*, can go to hell. I sang until 2:00 this morning. I am tired. I will sleep until 2:00 this afternoon if I wish, and I will *not* swim with you one more morning of my life. My walk is fine!" Then, astonishment again. "What do you mean 'pack'?"

His voice was businesslike. "We're going somewhere for a well earned rest" His voice did not reflect the anguish he felt over the order given by Carmine from Zio to take her away after her two week gig and see what might happen. Riddled with guilt, he had argued that it was too early for them to be alone together, she was not a woman to be pushed, he needed more time, anything. . .but to no avail. Zio's mind was set.

***

The sailboat looked very much like the one Lorgan owned, but, then, she had only seen his from afar so couldn't be sure the resemblance was intentional. It would make sense, though, that he would rent a boat similar to his own in order to feel at ease with it. The captain was stocking the galley with salamis, cheeses, fruits, steaks, eggs, whole black breads, tins of *fois gras*, wines, champagne, orange juice— The sloop could easily sleep six: two on the double bunk in the bow, two in the Master, and two in the galley where the bench seats folded up around the table to make a platform. She found scuba gear piled up near her bow bunk. When she opened the drawers assigned for her clothes, she found three new bathing suits, her size, already inside. Two bikinis and one tank suit. All white.

When the captain cast off, she turned, puzzled, to Lorgan. "What about Milo and the guys?"

Lorgan's heart sank. "We're going alone."

***

The captain had been gone for two days, so they actually were alone now, as Zio ordered. Lorgan only needed the Cap for the first stretch of the trip. Once they reached the British Virgins, he knew the waters and sailed himself, instructing her how to help by becoming his "first mate" because, as with his own boat, it took two to handle the sixty-foot sloop. They lounged now on a half moon of white sand beach that slipped gently into the sea from the nearby American island of St. John and, lunch over, finished their Scrabble game.

"I checked him out, and this Lou Roshard is young and rather new on the scene, but he seems legit. Quite a coincidence, though, his happening to be in the casino when you were."

Elyse watched Lorgan's hand as he rearranged Scrabble squares around on his little wood plank before making a new word on the board. The hand was browned from the sun. She remembered its surprising strength around her waist when he pulled her down from the parapet at his home.

"Are you Catholic?" she asked, touching the gold cross hanging around his neck. It was the only jewelry he wore.

"Yes," he captured a red, triple point square with his letters and garnered twenty-six points. "Aren't you?"

"No. Do you actually believe in God?" She placed her letters down on pink and got a Double. Still behind but not by much.

"Yes. Don't you?"

She watched his hand move the squares around again, searching for a combination. He held one of them for a long time, rubbing it sensuously between his fingers, thinking intently.

"No," she said, feeling his fingers pressed into her side again. "Nor Santa Claus or the Easter Bunny either."

***

When they went scuba diving, he resisted taking her outstretched hand as "buddies" might do, while they chased two Angel fish around a giant brain coral. She winked at him through her diving mask as he opened a sea urchin with his knife, which surrounded them instantly with hundreds of tiny, electric-blue fish fighting for its contents. He pretended not to notice. She felt light and weightless, as if they were flying high together in the sky, not swimming seventy-five feet beneath the surface of the ocean. He concentrated on providing activities to keep them busy as business colleagues taking a well-deserved break.

Back on the boat and removing their gear, he continued the morning's discussion, determined at all cost to keep their relationship professional. "What you do is express for your audience that which *they* can then feel from the song. You must always sing on a one-to-one basis, as if to each individual separately. The music is your indirect communication to which they respond or not from their subconscious mind. The lyric is your direct communication to which they respond with their conscious mind."

His black hair was tousled. It was the first time she'd ever seen it this way. It must look like this when he wakes up in the morning, she thought.

"That's why, even though your listeners may hold contradictions within themselves, you must never do it in your music. The words and the music must always complement each other to elicit an integrated response. There is nothing more emotionally upsetting or mentally confusing to a listener than affirmative music with negative lyrics. Think of 'The Impossible Dream' from Broadway's 'Man of La Mancha,' for example. The music is so beautiful and positive and uplifting, but the lyrics are full of wasted defiance, ending in despair and loss."

Elyse blanched. "The Impossible Dream? If you think that song is so upsetting because of its contradictions, why do you have it as a selection on your jukebox?"

Lorgan shrugged. "Because it reminds me. . ." His voice trailed off, and he got a pained, far-away look in his eyes. . . "of. . .things. . ."

She frowned. Something was up here, something important. *Something* about that particular song meant a great deal to him. She went over the lyrics in her mind, fragmented but best as she remembered them: *To dream the impossible dream. To fight the unbeatable foe. To bear with unbearable sorrow. . . To run where the brave dare not go. . . To love, pure and chaste from afar. To try, when you're arms are too heavy. To reach the unreachable star—This is my quest, to follow that star, no matter how hopeless, no matter how far. . ."* She couldn't remember any more, but these haunting, resignation-laden lyrics alongside the uplifting music were a signal that this was dangerous emotional territory far beyond his comfort zone. She would listen more closely next time she was in the cabana. Now she changed the subject quickly. "How did you get the name 'Lorgan'? I never heard it before."

"My mother named me after a big, heart-throb singer from the fifties when she was a kid. Tommy Lorgan. My mother is very musical and plays piano at a concert level."

"And your father?"

Lorgan looked far away again, into that deep, secret realm of his. "He does a variety of things. Business things."

But at other times, his eyes seemed a lighter shade for some reason down here in the Caribbean. They reflected the glittering, blue-green water. Elyse wasn't sure where she had been diving earlier in the morning. In the sea or in his eyes.

***

She beat the deck of the boat lightly with both hands, singing her own Calypso. Listening to an energetic old Jamaican man singing in a restaurant the night before she'd grown fascinated with the form. *Smoke your sweet pipe/And feel all right/Sip your water/and love your daughter.* "It's wonderful," she exclaimed. "It doesn't have to make sense, it just has to rhyme."

"The good ones make sense too," Lorgan argued. "That's the real talent in these old timers. They know how to make up words as they go along and develop a storyline at the same time." He watched her hands tapping rhythms. It must have been skin like hers that inspired all those trite descriptions of "honey-colored," he mused, but he was at a loss to come up with anything more original. Against his will, his eyes wandered up one arm and lingered on a bronze shoulder.

"What does *your* father do?" he asked, feeling suddenly perverse in order to shake off his unwanted, personal observations of her and curious as to what she would say.

Her hands never missed a beat. "He's in Venture Capital. Lends money to people for start-up businesses and things."

How very true, Lorgan thought. "Do you like him?" he asked.

"Not anymore." She beat out a complex, mixed rhythm. "Even as a child, I 'divorced' him a lot. When he thought I'd been a bad girl, he used to take away my toys and put them on top of his bureau. Since I was forbidden to touch anything there, I couldn't have them back until he decided I could. So I used to take a piece of paper and draw up a fancy certificate saying, "I. . ." she paused. "And then I put my initials, EG, hereby divorce, and then I put my father's name, as my father. Then I made him sign it and have my mother and a friend of my father's who was always around the house sign it as witnesses. They all thought it was very funny. When I was ten, I had copies made of the certificate, so I wouldn't have to draw up a new one every time."

"Why did you divorce him so often?"

"Because he took away my toys for silly reasons—he had

an unpredictable temper—and because when I was very young, he used to cut articles and pictures out of the newspaper. Our papers were periodically full of holes, and sometimes my favorite cartoon would be on the back of an article he wanted, and it would get cut away too."

"Why don't you like him now?"

Elyse laughed, her brown eyes teasing him. "Because he believes in God," she winked.

***

Her hair smelled of the sea and of flowers, the kind of which he couldn't identify. He resisted an insane desire to twirl the ends of it into his fingers as they danced. She had asked for the dance, so what could he do? He could see their boat nested with several others whose owners, like he and Elyse, were dining ashore on Peter Island. The boat he'd chosen to rent was nearly the same size and looked remarkably like his own, which made it easier for him to sail alone with her as an inexperienced helper. But he had never sailed *Dreamer* with a woman.

They were dancing a slow waltz. Elyse had learned extremely well. She felt light and graceful in his arms. She was whispering something in his ear. He wished she would stop. Her breath was warm and sweet.

"You know when I sing, I like to think that each man listening can imagine for a moment that I am singing to him alone. And that each woman listening can imagine she has some man to sing to."

"You must learn to always check the stage yourself," he said bringing the conversation back to a less personal level. "Be sure the lighting's right and never, ever sing a song you don't like."

The skin of her face smelled burned from the sun. One of her eyelashes brushed close to his mouth, irritating him.

They sat back down at their table and finished dinner. Elyse sipped her champagne pensively. "I think a singer must have the courage to bare her innermost values when she sings," she continued. "Don't you? Then you sing the words in a totally intimate way, and the whole performance gains a certain truth it could have no other way. Who's your favorite composer?" she asked, suddenly changing the subject.

"Wagner." Her coloring always reminded him of a sunset. Why? It disturbed him.

"Mine's Mozart. I love the intricacies of his melodies and the incredible sweetness of his harmonies. One would have to be in spiritual harmony with the universe itself to create harmonies like that."

Lorgan avoided the neckline of her gown. He had bought the gown for her, and she had worn it on one of her show nights in the Bahamas. He never noticed before that it was so low. Too low, he thought.

Elyse watched him as he seemed to study a brass chandelier. Probably thinking of lighting, she thought bitterly. He'd hardly noticed her all evening. So there really was no other reason for this trip except what he said. A "rest." She asked for more champagne not caring that she had drunk too much already.

NINE

HE COULD HEAR her turning restlessly on her bunk in the bow of the boat, as she had done for the past several nights now. He knew why, because he, too, had lain sleepless, only quieter, plagued by the irrepressible, irrational, increasing need to know whether she slept in a gown or not. Pajamas were clearly not her style, but maybe a gown? Maybe nothing?

Her bikinis were small. He had already seen most of her body: not skinny, flat-chested, and androgynous like most females her age, but full-bosomed, with a small waist, softly sculpted hips, and slim, shapely legs. How he hated himself for hungering to see the rest. Most of her was bronzed by the sun now, but the rest hidden beneath her bikinis would still be white, haloing—

This was not remotely according to plan. Lorgan opened his eyes quickly to abort the completion of his mental images. He hadn't counted on such a development in a million years. The sailing trip couldn't be avoided because it was ordered from the top, but he had felt certain he could keep everything between him and Elyse on an even, professional keel. Now he must consider the possibility that Zio's maniacal design was achieving itself in spite of his own noncooperation. Much as he wished otherwise, Elyse seemed to be passing beyond the girlish infatuation stage he had noticed earlier. During this last week of sailing he sensed a deepening of feeling in her eyes when she gazed at him. He heard it now in her insomnia. All he had countered against, protected against, was happening naturally with her? The infatuation stage was somewhat predictable because young performers often fell for their mentors, and he could handle that. But she seemed to be slipping into more mature emotions now? Worse, against all odds and against all possibilities he never anticipated these waves of desire in his own chest. Not this throbbing in his own loins. Not these images in his own mind. He never even *contemplated* this turn of events because from childhood he'd always been in complete control of his actions *and* his feelings.

He'd always been careful not to get involved seriously with any woman. He never would have considered a relationship with a woman connected to the Mob, and when in the few affairs he did have with "outsiders" he found himself on the brink of commitment, he broke off further advancement for fear of bringing an unsuspecting woman he cared for into his precarious world of Mobdom.

From the beginning he vowed never to bring *this particular* unsuspecting young woman into his bed, as Zio ordered. In fact, at all cost he vowed *never* to become personal with Elyse. And now, he didn't want to even more. Because he wanted so very much for her to be his on *honest* grounds, and this he knew was impossible. How had she unlocked him so? The unwitting minx! Full of feminine challenge but without a hint of coyness, she was somehow uncovering a buried but still burning passion and an unfulfilled sensuality within him. These were always there he supposed, expressed through "safe" choices like art and furnishings, but until Elyse he'd suppressed any risky emotions conveniently from his conscious mind and never released them fully with any woman. Because of her, his mind wasn't taking orders anymore.

Mother of God, he must be going mad thinking like this. It was all wrong. He had tried *not* to trick that softness into her eyes and tried *not* to plan the restlessness of her bed. She wasn't falling in love with *him* but with a false image of him, one her own evil father had fabricated for her. This he had vowed would *not* happen—

No, his body groaned silently in payment for the fraud against her. No. He couldn't do it. Not like this. He would tell her the truth tomorrow. He *must* tell her. He couldn't do this thing, even if it was real. Not to her. She was too good, too innocent.

Still, he couldn't bring himself to tell her tomorrow either. He was introducing her to Virgin Gorda, part of the British Virgin Islands just east of the American Virgins and the farthest reach of their trip. He must show it to her. Show her the most beautiful isle of them all, of any he had ever seen, even in Greece.

Great, giant boulders rose directly from the sea to shelter small stretches of white sand and create tiny, crystal-clear pools of water in between. The island was internationally well known, and the marina where they docked for the night was full of huge, luxury yachts from all over the world.

He had visited this haven many times alone. Each time, when he couldn't take the real world any longer, he booked into an exclusive resort here for a solitary rest. But the drama of the island's unique configuration drew him time and again into fuller explorations beyond the perimeters of the hotel complex until he found "The Baths," as this area was called. Its physical grandeur with the clear pools of water and the great ocean spreading out endlessly beyond was like a magical sanctuary to cleanse both body and soul from the filth of the rest of the real world. He always felt refreshed and renewed after spending time in this perfect place, a place where one could hide all alone and privately dream of things better than they are. *Impossible dreams*, perhaps, but inspiring just the same, even if they never could become real.

Tomorrow morning, he was taking Elyse to one special, God-kissed beach he discovered many years ago. He could not tell her the truth before offering her this paradise. It would be a going away present from him, its beauty offered as a sacrifice upon the altar of their unfortunate births.

Because she would surely hate him and leave him after he confessed he had been ordered by her father to mount her career. And what would Zio do to him if he learned he crossed The Boss? Who knew? Valuable as he was to California, given Zio's temper, his own life might not be worth the price of a postcard upon their return. Mother of God! What a mess! Lorgan pressed his mouth deeper into his pillow. In honor of her talent, her independence, her courage, he *must* tell her! He would tell her tomorrow *night*. He *would* do it. But he must have one last day first. Tomorrow.

***

She posed for him in one of her bikinis, rising up to her toes on top of the small mountains of smooth stone, leaning lazily against their sloping sides, slithering slowly into rock-carved basins of clear water, lifting her sun-kissed red hair to the warm fragrance of the air. Lorgan snapped photographs of her from the sand.

After an early morning sail, they anchored the boat out from The Baths and swam ashore just before dawn, towing the dingy full of food and photographic equipment, so Lorgan could get some casual shots of her in a bathing suit. He told her these informal photos would accompany a feature article in a fashion magazine and that professional photos in evening gowns and daywear would be taken later.

She prepared their bacon and eggs over a fire he built, frying their black bread in a mixture of bacon grease and butter and, of course, accompanying their breakfast with champagne and orange juice. They dawdled around from one little pool to another after breakfast, and now she played by herself, dancing dripping wet here and there among the rock formations. Last night's decision inspired him to bring along the camera and fabricate the fashion-spread lie. At least he would have pictures of her by which to remember this idyllic week. To remember her. . .if Zio let him live even on memories.

Suddenly, he stopped clicking the camera, his eyes fixed in shocked stillness on the viewfinder.

Elyse had thrown off her bathing suit and was standing still, defiant and inviting, completely nude before him.

He continued, momentarily stunned by her beauty, by her impulsiveness, by her audacity, to stare mesmerized through the lens of his camera as she walked slowly but deliberately toward him. He felt the camera being wrenched from his hands and the heat of her mouth at the same time. Then they fell to the carpet of sand together as he, in spite of his vows, answered her demands by taking command.

Suddenly he stopped in disbelief, meeting a resistance he never expected. She smiled up at him. "No one ever deserved me before," she said simply.

Lorgan felt a jolt of unbearable pressure in his chest as denial rocked him from within. As if *he* deserved her? Then, studying her face intently for a long moment and staking their lives on the decision, he gathered her to him again, this time with infinite gentleness, before lifting her into his arms and carrying her to another spot of sand, one secluded and protected by the huge, gray boulders. Laying her carefully on the ground, he abandoned all caution and covered her body tenderly with kisses, with caresses, with words, with his own body until hers forgot its barrier, until her desire for him was so great she didn't notice that her pleasure contained pain. Her final cry of ecstasy hurled him back to the first moments he saw her, throwing her head back with the same free, uninhibited primal sound at the end of her song. His own low moans became the echoing chords beneath her crescendo, as he sucked away a spot of blood that had appeared on her lip at the same moment the blood of her innocence disappeared into the sand. He buried his face in her breasts. "God help us, Mother of God forgive me," he breathed. "I love you."

He lifted her again and carried her—a truly innocent treasure in every unimaginable way to be protected, cherished, safeguarded—to a small pool of water, and sitting on a rock at its edge slowly and gently bathed her body with cool sea water. The sun kissed their feet with the promise of a clear day, and he looked into her face to see the sunrise.

***

Back on the boat, Elyse lay the entire night nestled in his arms, as she had dreamed of doing with a loved one for so long, postponing and postponing, and postponing again and again her first time until the absolutely right man came along. Now, she stretched her body out full length until every surface of it touched some part of Lorgan. His breathing was even, and she smiled contentedly as he kissed her hair softly from time to time in his sleep.

He loved her body, she knew, the same way he loved her music. Because they were one and the same. The same source, only different expressions of her mind, her soul, her *her*. And over many months, she had grown to love him as she always believed it was possible to love. Slowly, and then. . .completely.

She often berated herself for waiting, for insisting upon waiting for the right man. It was unthinkable to be a twenty-two-year-old virgin graduating from college. Then a twenty-three and twenty-four-year-old. And, finally, a twenty-five-year-old. Now, she was glad she waited. Lorgan was worth the wait.

She'd thought for a time when she was in college that she was in love with Nico. She wanted to be in love with him, even though he was two years her junior. Age hadn't mattered then, as it didn't matter now that Lorgan was nearly twice her age. But it *had* mattered when Nico found out about her Family and tossed what he learned so cruelly in her unsuspecting face. He never imagined she didn't know. He'd been sorry afterward, but it was too late. They remained close friends, but she could never love him after that.

She wondered if her mother still loved her father. Doria hadn't known of her husband's Mob activities either. It was hard to believe at first. Elyse felt certain that many Mob wives knew about their husbands. How could one not know on some level? But that was just it. Her mother was European-born, in northern rather than southern Italy, and brought up in a convent her entire life. Of all people, she wouldn't suspect. And since Zio cut out all mention of any person she might recognize from all publications coming into the house, it was virtually impossible for her to learn after they were married. In addition, this was a new age for the *La Cosa Nostra*. Even though they suffered exposure now and then and especially those few years ago with all the raids, they had successfully for several decades kept their activities under cover of legitimate businesses. Unlike their fathers before them, their internal wars were carried out subtly and out of the spotlight.

Her mother had certainly loved her father once. Of that Elyse held no doubt. She remembered as a young child, seeing them dressed up for one of their many evenings dining and jazz clubbing in Manhattan. Their social life seemed so glamorous to her young eyes. Both her parents were beautiful, her mother's long, red hair twisted into ringlets and scattered with fresh flowers, and her handsome father clasping a diamond necklace around his wife's neck and draping furs gently around her shoulders. They appeared so affectionate with each other that little Elena had waited with unbearable impatience to grow up and share evenings like that with a man of her own. She and her mother both knew, now, as neither of them ever suspected then, with what kinds of people her parents socialized during those extravagant evenings in the city. And she knew, now, what kind of men had always been her babysitters. Men she adored, who made lasagna and smelled of garlic, which made her giggle then. But men who carried guns, which made her cringe now.

At last all of that was over. It was another life, behind her now. She possessed a man of her own, one she had longed and long-waited for. And he was as clean and strong and gentle as existed in this world. How wonderful to sleep with a man. At what other time in one's life was one so vulnerable? What enormous, implicit trust there was in the simple act of a man and a woman sleeping together. What a wondrous thing to share with someone you love, the ordinary routine of greeting each day together.

A whole new world awaited her. She had waited and waited, but now it was hers. Eventually, she would tell Lorgan about her father, but she felt certain he would understand that "Zio" had nothing to do with her. It wasn't that she felt afraid to tell him. It just wasn't the time. It was time, instead, to forget all bitterness of the past, all lingering disappointments with her Family. Lorgan was her world now. He would take care of her. They would take care of each other.

Putting one hand on his cheek and snuggling into the protectiveness of his arms, she fell asleep without dreaming, for her most important dream had come true.

TEN

SOUNDS OF THE SMALL orchestra warming up filled the studio. Nico had arrived before them. Elyse whispered to Lorgan as they crossed the room to where he stood: "I want you to meet my closest friend. I invited him because we've been together a long time, through a lot together, and I want him here to share this day with me." She looked up happily into Lorgan's eyes. "And I want him to meet you."

Nico returned Lorgan's warm handshake with a cold smile and handed him his Blogger business card. "Lorgan Cantrell." He said. "Any relation to Tommy Lorgan of the old days?"

Lorgan laughed. "No, but you've done your homework. My mother named me after that singer."

"Cantrell. What kind of name is that? Italian? Cantrelli?"

Elyse shot a stern glance at Nico. *Get off it*, her eyes warned her obsessive friend. Nico got the message and started asking Lorgan about the recording session. Satisfied and seeing Lou, she left Lorgan and Nico alone and skipped over to discuss the orchestra with her producer. "Lou, I really don't want any electronic sounds in there. I hate those sounds—"

Lou looked nervously up to the control room and sipped milk from a paper cup. "Whatever ya say, Baby. You no want electronic sounds, you no got 'em."

Without Elyse nearby, Nico went back to grilling Lorgan. "Can't figure where 'Cantrell' comes from unless it comes from 'Cantrelli'. But the only Cantrellis I know of are Carmine, who runs gambling junkets to Europe and the Caribbean, and Frankie, who's under periodic investigation by the Feds."

"Never heard of them," Lorgan smiled thinly and, bowing slightly, removed himself from any further inquiry. After they became lovers, he still hadn't summed up the nerve to tell Elyse about her father's orders. Riddled with guilt and burdened with the knowledge that he must tell her, the big question was *when*. He couldn't risk upsetting her first professional recording, but this friend of hers sounded pretty savvy, maybe even suspicious—

He walked up to Elyse in her sound booth, where she was listening to the orchestra rehearse. He made a small correction on one of her charts and, without fanfare, handed her a plain white box tied with a white satin ribbon.

"Oh!" she smiled wide with delight.

"It will help you sing better," he smiled back.

She lifted the gardenia from its tissue and held it briefly to her nose. Then she kissed it softly and touched it to his cheek.

Lou came hurrying up to them, unaware he was interrupting a private moment. "Come on, Baby. We gotta get this show on the road. I got important people up there in the control room watching you today, Baby."

Lorgan and Elyse looked up toward the large control

room window above them but could discern no one inside because of the glare from the lights. "Who's up there?" Lorgan asked.

"My new partner," Lou answered quickly, draining the last of his milk and tossing the cup into a trash barrel. "Big money. Gonna do a lot for this gal."

Lorgan turned to Elyse and pulled her to him for one brief moment, his eyes shining with an inner light that was steady now. She saw it every day, an open declaration of his love. "Sing for me, darling," he whispered. Then he released her to her jittery producer.

Her sounds came from deeper now. They came richer. She had crossed the line to full womanhood in the past few weeks, and it showed in her voice. It showed in her stance. It showed in her eyes. Elyse Gannon was not only a superb singer. She was also a radiant woman.

The orchestra caught her high-spirited delivery and supported it without reserve. She sent a quick, warm wink to Milo and Bill and Louis and Bobby, all of them participating for the first time in a full orchestral production. Then she sang to Lorgan.

They cut her own compositions first. "Butterfly." "Heroes." "This is my Man." "Can You Come out and Play Today?" "The World's a Sweet Balloon."

Her energy beamed like a laser into the musicians. She pulled it endlessly out of herself, inspiring them to gather it enthusiastically into their own performances. They were all flying high together. Not one of them heard the music they were making with their ears alone. They felt it in the very center of their beings because their souls were alive in the music. Because she was so magnetic, instrumentalists she didn't even know turned themselves inside out, performing to the best of their ability to make this first recording session an especially good one for her.

Lorgan sat listening intently, finding it difficult to remain objective. The music was so positive and uplifting, so unlike most of what was offered in most of today's depressing music world. Mother of God help them. Because she was so good, might they actually have a chance to rise above and beyond the Mob? What luck Lou happened to be in the audience down in the Bahamas and so unknown they could do this recording unnoticed by anyone of import. He could never otherwise have cut a disc with an orchestra for Elyse without Zio's interference. Zio was too on top of him at every turn now. Even if he used his own, normal orchestral connections, Zio would insist on approving each move to advance her career. This way, unexpectedly, he might be able to extricate them from the built-in *Cosa Nostra* web in which they both were caught by releasing the recording quickly through his regular, reliable PR people and let it sail on its own without "help." His only continuing hope was that because she was unique, she actually might be able to find a public by herself. If she managed that, they could try to take off alone on her success and, if they were lucky, leave the Mob behind. Then he would *never* have to tell her—

He'd checked Roshard out several times in several different ways. The young, hipster guy turned out to be just what he said: a one-man operation run out of his New York apartment with a few modest successes in the Rock field. Elyse was a new and mature step for him, and he seemed just right for her. Now Lou evidently had a new, big-money partner. What could be better?

Mother of God, he turned his attention back to the music. How she got that cry of joy into both her music and her lovemaking he would never know. And he would never care, as long as it was there.

They wrapped early. Everyone was exhausted, but the tired grins on their faces were not from weariness. They gave tribute to a most satisfying day of work.

The music, hours ago, dissolved Nico's aggressiveness. He shook his head dazedly as if waking from a trance and walked toward Lorgan to make amends for his earlier, nasty attitude by complimenting him on the superb session. He never heard Elyse sing so elegantly, and she did not hide the fact that she sang to only one man in the room.

Engineers left for the day. Lights in the control room went off. Musicians wandered randomly out the heavy, sound-padded door.

Although still some distance from Lorgan and in a different area of the huge sound stage, Nico stopped short. From his own vantage point Lorgan looked up at exactly the same moment. Totally unaware of each other's sudden fixation on that door, the same item caught both of their attentions: A white handkerchief peeking out from the breast pocket of a dark blue suit worn by an elderly man, who quickly descended the steps from the control room and walked briskly from the studio.

Nico looked from Lorgan to Elyse, who was lying across a row of chairs, dabbing her face with a wet paper towel. He had the answer to his questions.

Lorgan stared at the now-closed door, frowning deeply. His questions were just beginning.

ELEVEN

LORGAN WROTE IN longhand, so when the time came, she would recognize his handwriting.

My Elyse,

From this day forward until I don't know when, I shall write the truth to you in this manner. I meant to tell you these things on Virgin Gorda, but after we became lovers, I could not bring myself to do it. I was hoping beyond hope that we could escape our destinies. Now, I shall continue to lie to you and betray you each day until this horrible scenario is played out, but for my own sanity I must have some way of letting you know that I am not a willing party to these happenings. As events unfold, which I cannot tell you about yet, I shall write them down like this and mail them registered, numbered, dated, and sealed to a secure post office box so that one day in the future you will believe me when I tell you I am not a willing player in this chess game that uses you as its unsuspecting pawn. I am but another pawn.

I met with your father this morning when you thought I was visiting my cousin Jason in L.A., and he confirmed that he is a major shareholder in "Deco Discs," Lou Roshard's recording company. There is nothing I can do about this except swear to you that I didn't know about it when we signed contracts with Lou. They are keeping certain of their plans from me, now. Do they suspect I have fallen honestly, eternally in love with you and will try to extricate us from their clutches? Perhaps they do. I don't know how they would, but I must be extra careful in all dealings with them in order to protect both of us.

Tonight I shall tell you the wonderful news that we have been approached by some people to whom I sent a demo of your CD, and we shall soon open a new nightclub in Chicago for them. But I confess to you, here, that which I cannot confess tonight. The club is a front for your half-brother Paulie. Behind the club will be another kind of club. One with mindless blobs for members, cowardly escapees from the real world, who cannot face it no matter what their background or social status. It will be a club for animals. No, worse: it will be a club for sub-humans, who in place of a hat will check their brains at the door.

Even in the main club, the jukebox that plays your songs when you are not singing in person will be owned and run by a group of your father's organization, along with the Chicago Family. The laundry will be picked by another and the garbage by another. The meat served at dinner will be provided for the restaurant by another of the "Family," the fruits and vegetables by another. The limousine service that deposits your "public" at the club's entrance is owned by your father's friends, as is the bank that will finance the project. As am I, my dearest love. As are you.

If I resist, they will threaten you. You must believe this. Your father is renowned for his temper. Therefore, I shall comply for the time being. I am alone in this. I cannot tell you anything yet, for you, understandably, would not believe me, or if you did, you would despise me for life. Except for that last crushing raid and the incarceration of dozens of La Cosa Nostra from top to bottom of the organization, neither you nor I would be of any interest to your father. The general public has again forgotten the Mob's existence because for years the "Families" have been careful to keep all activities under the public radar, and even though the collateral damage to the Mob from that raid goes on, average people are too busy with their technological toys to care about the real world any longer. It's because of unrest within the Mob that your father needs to choreograph your career in order to bring you back to the Family.

It is my desperate hope that once your album is released to the public, once you perform in this new club, once serious music lovers become aware of you, that you alone can lift both of us out of this hell. As in Communist countries, once dissidents become well known to the big world, it is harder to do away with them.

Elyse, your mother is a dying woman inside. She is powerless to save you, but I want you to know that these actions on the part of your father are killing her. I can see it in her eyes. Forgive us both, my darlingheart, for our weaknesses. We have been wrong to remain silently with these vermin all these years. But I declare to you that we both love you.

Yours forever,
Lorgan

He sealed the envelope and pressed it against his lips for a moment, hoping she would never have to read it. Then he put the letter in his jacket pocket and headed for the post office.

TWELVE

"OH, JESUS, GOD-A-MIGHTY, go all to hell, man. Get away from here. You think I can be seen with a reporter coming into my apartment?"

Nico pushed his way in through the partially opened door. "Then shut the door. I have to talk to you."

Lou looked up and down the hallway and, seeing no one, closed the door, leaning heavily against it. "I just hope nobody saw you come into the lobby, man. Wasn't the doorman there? Nobody rang up about a visitor. What the hell do you want?"

Nico walked over to Lou's bar and poured them both a straight scotch. The two young men had exchanged cards when they met at Elyse's recording session, so Nico was able to come over to Lou's place straightaway for this urgent conversation. "I came in through the garage and took the service elevator, so don't worry. Besides, nobody recognizes a mere Blogger. I just took the precautions out of habit. Now you have to tell me straight, Lou. I know that Rinaldo Gadonni is a partner in your company. What I need to know is if you want him to be. I hear you drink only milk, but I think you better take this."

Lou downed the scotch, wincing at its bite, but poured himself another, glad now that he kept his bar well stocked for visitors. "What's it to *you*?"

Nico sipped slowly at his own drink. He intended to stay in Lou's apartment until he found out what he needed to know. "Number one: 'Elyse Gannon' is the professional name of 'Elena Gadonni'." He noted the genuine shock registering on Lou's face. Okay. He didn't know about that. "Right," he continued. "Zio's daughter. Number two: Zio's father, Dino, had my grandfather killed when my father was still a young boy, so I have a *very* personal score to settle. Understand?"

Lou nodded and topped off his drink. He needed it badly.

"When my grandfather was young, he had three close friends: Dino Gadonni, Frank Cantrelli, Sr., and another guy of no importance to this conversation. As kids, they ran numbers together up in the Bronx, drove pick-up cars, and collected for shylocks in the Mob. It didn't mean a thing then because they were young and because every kid in the neighborhood was doing the same thing. It was later that it got to matter."

Nico took the bottle from Lou's hand. "Sit down, Lou. Nobody's going to hurt you tonight, this may take awhile, and you're not used to hard liquor." Lou sat down on the living room couch, reluctantly nursing his existing drink.

"You have to understand that until Prohibition, there was no real *organized* crime in America. It was a local thing, small gangs of many different ethnic origins scattered all over the country, one gang having no official connection to another. It was during and after Prohibition—and because of it—that they became connected. Because with that legislative Amendment against alcohol, there grew a *need* for criminals to organize. Smuggling booze into America was not a multi-gang job. Whole fleets of ships, huge convoys of trucks, warehouses, island bases off Newfoundland, even armed planes were eventually used to channel the flow of illegal alcohol from Canada, Europe and the Caribbean into the United States.

"It was prohibition, too, that popularized crime in America. The gangs that brought them illegal gin were cheered on by the citizens of the country. Instead of publicly condemning the *law*, Americans made heroes out of the law-*breakers*, guys like Al Capone and Lucky Luciano for example. They became famous instead of infamous.

"Millions upon millions of dollars were made, but at the same time the whole underworld trying to work together for the first time was in ferment. Organization called for leadership. Blood was spilled daily as gangs and individual members clawed their way to the top. Rinaldo's father was young and unknown at the time, but he was smart, quick to grasp an opportunity, and he was making barrels of money hijacking other mobster's boatloads of booze. Killings at sea were easily disposed of in 'cement coffins', which were just barrels stuffed with bodies and cement and dumped into the water, but later he hijacked trucks as well and began to have trouble getting rid of the bodies discreetly.

"My grandfather worked in a funeral home. Dino and Frank, who were partners by then, forced him to do their dirty work by using what they called a 'double-decker coffin', which had a false bottom so they could hide the body of a criminal below a legitimate dead person's body in the casket just before burial. After awhile, my grandfather couldn't take it. He couldn't stomach the fact that his former friends were robbing and killing people on a wholesale scale, even if most of the victims were criminals themselves. Plus, they were exploiting others, extorting, torturing, and tormenting all who got in their way—mobsters, speakeasy owners, on-lookers—it didn't matter. He went to the authorities.

"The next thing my father knew, he was visiting the funeral home where *his* father worked. And his own father was the star corpse. They had filled his head with buckshot, and he'd crashed into dozens of vases full of peonies when he fell. My father saw him that way, lying among hundreds of white flowers sprayed with the red of his blood. Later, two years after I was born, my father committed suicide. My mother vanished. I was raised by my grandmother, who had lost both husband and son to the Mob. She was a strong and wonderful woman. She is now dead, too, but just from old age."

Lou's head shot up, shock and pain warring for an expression on his face.

"Yeah," Nico said in a low voice. "That's why I'm a Mafia-exposing Blogger with no impact but a lot of passion. But I digress. Let's get back to history.

"After the repeal of Prohibition and many gang wars, Rinaldo's father rose through the ranks to become, the 'first among firsts' in New York and the head of the strongest Family, which also headed the four other New York Families. Dino married a Naples girl and had three children by her. Rinaldo was the oldest. He supplied services people wanted. Services some people will always want, and services that will always create crime as long as any government makes the goods and services illegal. He supplied lots of other things, too, like torture and bullets. He was a ruthless killer. Anyone, and I mean *anyone*, who got in his way was quickly put 'out of the way.'

"By the time Rinaldo came of age, everything was set for him to take over, and he kept his father's activities going full speed: drugs, prostitution, illegal gambling, extortion, murder—lots of murder. He became a *made member* before his twentieth birthday. *Zio*, as he likes to be called—'uncle'—is his father's son in every manner, right from his pitiless temperament to his stupid suits and stupid breakfasts. It was only after his first wife died and he married the little convent girl who would become Elyse's mother that he began infiltrating legitimate businesses—dress shops, liquor stores, apartment buildings, all sorts of things—businesses where he always had a piece of the profits but never had a piece of the losses.

"Which, I believe, my gullible friend, brings us in quick, abbreviated form to the present subject of *your* legitimate business. But who needs details? I'm sure you got punched in the ears with details. Now, I've told you my story. You tell me yours."

"Can I have another drink?"

"Sure. It's your apartment."

"I never met the old man until Elyse's recording session. Only his son." Lou poured himself another scotch but added some ice and water this time. His stomach was rebelling, but his nerves still begged for calm.

Nico looked at Lou sternly. He couldn't let him back down now. He had to make him tell it. "Reno?" he demanded.

"Yeah, I think he's beginning to run things now that his father's getting older."

"Right," Nico agreed. "At least at the operational level. He's now Underboss."

"Well, I always liked the fun of gambling, not big time,

but still. . . Anyway, Reno was the one who came to me after I defaulted on a gambling loan. No, that's not quite right. A couple other guys visited me first. I was behind, see, on this loan I got from a black guy in Harlem. A friend of mine told me about him, and look, I've seen enough movies to know what loan sharks are all about. But I knew I needed the money for only a real short time, and since I was so young with no collateral, the bank wouldn't give me any."

"And what else did you need the money for?"

Lou groaned, caught. "This chick. She was a hot, soul-singer chick, see? And I didn't want to lose the chance to be the one to launch her career, so I recorded her with the borrowed money."

"So? What else?"

"So the chick marries her high school dropout boyfriend and won't do any gigs, and what the hell, sounds corny as hell, right, but that's what happened."

"They all sound corny."

"After I missed only three payments, these grease balls take me out to lunch at some place down in Little Italy to see what we can work out. Right there at the table, they started beating me. They slugged me till I was bleeding from my nose and my mouth, and then they stopped and ordered me a cup of coffee. I am tellin' you, man, everybody in that whole restaurant saw everything and never stopped shoveling spaghetti. There are tourists all over the place in Little Italy these days, but that didn't stop them. Then after coffee, they beat me again. This time my ears were bleeding, my eyes were beginning to close up, and my jaw was out of commission. I couldn't talk for three days. Then they ordered me another cup of coffee and left the restaurant. They told me to have the money by the next day and somebody would be by my apartment to pick it up.

"Well, I tried all night to dig up money. But nobody I knew had that much or could get it so soon. Yeah, man. I was stupid. I was only in for ten grand, but after all their astronomical 'interest charges' were added to that pretty small loan, I was in to them for sixty-some grand by then. Pure extortion, ya know?

"It was three days later that Gadonni's son, Reno, came here to the apartment. He informed me that his father was my new partner and I had a new client: Elyse Gannon. I told him I'd pay back my debts but my business wasn't for sale. Then he started raving like a madman. Shouted I was stupid. *'Everything's* for sale! Everything's a war,' he screamed. Man! He was nuts gone bonko! Said maybe he liked war, but he didn't invent it. He ranted on about politicians with their pinkies in the till. Cops who handed out more beatings than his own thugs. Lawyers and judges? He'd buy me one for Christmas. Said things are not right or wrong. Just smart or stupid. He was, like, crazy. Then he—" Lou stopped talking and looked longingly at the bar.

"I know," Nico said. "They tagged him *Reno The Piranha.* All mobsters have a handle that suits their personality or their M.O. Some are funny. His isn't."

"Yeah. . ." Lou drawled, remembering. He set his empty glass down on the coffee table. "When I kept telling him I didn't *have* the money and didn't know where to get it so fast, he pulled a plastic bag out of his coat pocket. It had water and a couple little fish in it. He took the fruit out of that bowl on the table right there, dumped the plastic bag into it, water and all, and called one of his flunkies over. The guy started sweating and shaking and whining in kind of a puppy sort of way, begging Reno to forgive him for. . .I don't know what. He just kept whimpering that he would never do it again. So scaring me was clearly only part of the play. The guy must've done something awful to get that punishment.

Anyway—Oh, God-a-mighty, man—that flunky finally put his hand in that bowl, and, oh God, man—"Lou doubled over holding his stomach. "Oh my God! Those fish ate the tip of one of his fingers off faster than a wink. I signed the papers bringing them into my business right then and there." Lou staggered to his feet, his face red and sweating, his stomach churning like holy hell. He was half-crying. "Now get outta here, man! Get outta here! I had no choice. I went to the Bahamas and did everything they told me to do. And Jesus Christ, of all things, the girl is good. They never needed to fix it— They never needed—"

Nico felt like crying himself. He poured them both a small topper and guided Lou gently back to the couch. Sitting next to him, he put one arm around the poor guy's slumped-over shoulders. "Lou, Buddy, you have to tell this to the right people."

THIRTEEN

SHE SNUGGLED CLOSE to him in the cab on the way into town from O'Hare airport. They had flown to New York three days ago for final fittings of her gowns and a fresh haircut by the only stylist Lorgan would let near her. Los Angeles was full of designers and hair stylists, but Lorgan would have none of the flashy Hollywood "look" so insisted on the understated elegance of New York. She'd marveled from the beginning at how he lavished financial outlay and detailed attention on her but assumed that's how things were done Big Time. Now he was going well beyond that. Was it because he believed in her talent so much? Or was it because they were lovers now? Did it matter?

"There's a surprise waiting for you at the club," he said.

"I can't wait to see it!"

"The surprise or the club?"

"Both."

It had been a wildly busy but supremely happy four months in preparation for an opening like this one. She was still in shock that Lorgan was able to book such a serious gig for her so early in her career let alone a new, posh Chicago nightclub. She wasn't sure she really believed it yet. It all seemed too good to be true.

Lorgan had flown back and forth between Chicago and California a few times to finalize business arrangements and make subtle suggestions for staging set-ups as he watched the progress of the club's renovation take shape. She composed two new songs, mostly in his absence, and loved staying in his dramatic, cliff-top home without him. It seemed almost more intimate than when he was there; plus, she became extra friendly with the dogs as she cared for them while he was gone.

When there together, they found time to sail "Dreamer" many times. She was becoming a good "First Mate," and it was a relaxing diversion for both of them from the strenuous work to get her ready for a major opening like this. On those precious afternoons, they packed sandwiches and drove a half-mile down the hill from his home to the beach where Lorgan kept his small dingy, which was the only way to get out to the big sloop, and after a sail and a swim, enjoyed a leisurely few hours lunching and loving. They shared their passion for music and their passion for each other. It was all that they needed.

But when alone, she also listened carefully time and time again to "The Impossible Dream." There was something she still didn't understand about this song and why it was included in the jukebox collection. A feeling of yearning permeated the song, but there *was* a disconnect between the positive, soaring music and the lyrics of loss and despair, which defied his lectures about their necessity to be in harmony with each other. There did seem to be one common denominator however: Beyond the general tone of yearning, there also seemed to be a desperate striving, a striving toward something more and a belief that a better world existed but remained always out of reach for some unfathomable reason she couldn't grasp.

The guys would be flying out to California next week to join her for final rehearsals. They—and the club—were almost ready. Today Lorgan was stopping for an overnight in Chicago before flying on to California, and she was going to get her first look-see at the club, so she would know exactly what to expect when she came out for the opening itself.

Lorgan sat back in his seat, rubbed her thigh gently, and sang: "The World's a sweet balloon, toss it in the air, turn it in your hand, the world is round and wonderful—"He stopped singing. "Oh, by the way, you've got your first TV guest spot coming up. The Sam Jamison show. His late-night gig is only syndicated here in the mid-west, but it's a start. Sam's an old friend, and he's having you on as a favor to me. You'll do it live here a couple of days before the opening, so we need to decide which song you'll sing. You'll get only one. He's got a big following."

Elyse covered him with kisses. "The only thing, Lorgan, is. . . Don't you think I ought to attend some of these business meetings? I mean, you're doing everything, and I really don't understand very much about how these things are done when the venue is an important one. In Cleveland, the guys and I just played our gigs at local bars for very little pay and took home the extras that customers put into the brandy snifter on the piano. This is a big jump up for all of us, especially me."

"That's why I'm bringing you here before the gig, so you'll be familiar with everything and not be nervous later. As for business issues, it's my job to do all that negotiating and paper work, darling. I'm your manager."

Elyse frowned. "I know, but I feel I ought to learn about other aspects of my career, too. Maybe I don't have to, but I'd like to. I mean you even select my gowns—"

"Lorgan!" Elyse leaned over him suddenly, as the cab rounded the corner near the club. A long, deep-purple limousine was just pulling away from the curb ahead of them.

"What's the matter?" Lorgan's voice had a sharp edge to it. He'd spotted Paulie's car, too. God damn him! Paulie was supposed to stay away from the club until it was finished. He was also ordered by Zio to stay out of sight until Elyse's two-week gig was over because Zio couldn't afford to have any clues around to alert Elyse as to who really set her up so unexpectedly in such a hot spot. Zio hired the architect for the elegant, new drug den and financed the whole project for his son, so little weakling *Paulie The Professor* had no reason to be in on the construction of it anyway. What was he doing here? Probably just strutting around, acting like the big shot he would never be. God damn him!

Elyse sat back, frowning deeply, thinking hard. It couldn't be! But Nico said her half-brother was expanding his drug bars from New York to Chicago— No, it couldn't be. The coincidence was too great!

"Elyse, what's the matter?" Lorgan asked urgently. He had to play the game at least for the next few weeks, didn't he? Maybe not? Mother of God, should he tell her *now*? But knowing her fierce independence and willfulness, if he did, she most definitely would refuse to sing. He *had* to let her open and wait for the right time for both of them to get free. Mother of God, what a mess.

Elyse looked at him, shaking her head in bewilderment. "No," she said slowly, her brain reeling. "I thought I saw someone I know getting into that limo. But it couldn't be. . . Never mind."

"Who did you think you saw?"

"Nobody important. Never mind." She hadn't told Lorgan about her Family yet. She'd better do it soon, she thought. Accidental meetings do happen, and Nico did say Paulie was moving to Chicago. It would be better if Lorgan were prepared. Once the club opened, it was certainly possible Paulie might come to one of her shows if only out of curiosity to see her perform. It was just the unusual color of the limo that had thrown her, the same crazy purple as Paulie's. She hadn't really had a good look at who was getting into it—forget it. "Come on," she said brightly, dismissing the subject. "Show me my present."

They walked past workmen, who were putting up the entrance façade. The place was nearly finished. Beautiful even during the day, it would be magnificent at night with soft lights bathing the midnight-blue carpeting and setting off the walls of soft blue-gray and the peach velvet booths surrounding tables of glass and chrome. Very Retro-Deco but with a clean, minimalist lack of ornamentation that added a futuristic element to it all. The blue of the ceiling was so deep it was almost black, studded with hundreds of tiny pinpoints of lights that would become distant stars at night. Elyse shook her head in wonderment. And *she* was going to open *this* club? Definitely too good to be true— Then she saw it, raised on a stage at the far end of the room. "Oh no! Lorgan!" She ran to the Lucite piano and stood before it, shaking her bowed head, her long copper-red hair swinging from side to side, her face frozen into stunned astonishment by the tumult of emotions rising wave after wave through her entire body. This was *all* too good to be true—

Lorgan came up close behind her, and turning her around, lifted her chin with his hand. His eyes were glistening, as were hers. "It's yours," he smiled. "It belongs to you. After your engagement here, I'll have it shipped back home, where I've rented a regular one to finish rehearsing, but I wanted you to have it to sit on for your *big* opening night, and I wanted you to see it here ahead of time, right where you'll be. It arrived only yesterday."

"Lorgan, I love you, you know," she said, smiling back at him.

"Yes, I know."

She pulled him over to a ringside table and sat him down. Then, grabbing a workman's wrench from one of the tables as she passed by, she skipped to the stage and hiked herself up onto the piano. "Guess who I wrote this one for." And she sang to him, using the tool as if it were a microphone.

This is my man
In his hands the touch that sets me free
My man
In his smile the joy that lets me see a secret part of me
This is my man—
This is my love
In his eyes an understanding deep
My love
In his kiss a soft commanding heat, a warmth that I can keep
This is my love...

Some of the men working outside wandered into the room and stood at the entrance listening. Nods of appreciation passed between them as Elyse graciously included them into her private audience and sang to them as well. She felt enough love at this moment to share it with the entire world.

Once he was a dream
A dream that I could hold against the days that left me weeping
But now I turn my head at night if I'm afraid and see the real
man by me sleeping
It's our light, so it seems, that fires the morning cold
Before the dawning sun can reappear
And storms have only led to promises remade
They failed to cool our fire with tears

These are my years
In his arms the dizziness of wine
My years
In his heart the future beats in time with every beat of mine
These are my years
This is my year, this is my love, this is my. . .Man

The workers continued to watch when, the song over, the man sitting near the stage walked over to the piano and, lifting the woman down into his arms, kissed her lengthily.

"I have to go see some people about your publicity," he murmured into her hair. "Why don't I leave you here to check out your dressing room and things, then you grab a taxi and I'll meet you at the hotel in an hour or so for lunch. Okay?"

"But Lorgan," Elyse protested. "That's just the sort of thing I was talking about on the way here in the cab. I want to be in on some of these meetings. I mean, I'd like to learn how you play everything out in the business world in order to be such a wizard! Like Dorothy landing suddenly in OZ from Kansas, I feel I'm not in Cleveland anymore but wonder just how I got *here* so fast."

"It wouldn't be professional," Lorgan countered. "That's what you have a *business* manager for, trust me." He kissed her again, lightly this time, and walked quickly out the door.

Elyse wandered into the Ladies' and Men's rooms. Cute. Similar to little Speakeasy entrances she'd seen in old movies, each stall was made up of four doors with tiny windows in them that in the old days of Prohibition were opened by some bouncer on the other side to hear a password that would admit customers into the rooms serving illegal liquor. Here, the windows were mirrors. The doors looked real, though, complete with handles and hinges. She tried one. Fake. Cute idea though, and it carried out the underlying Art Deco design theme of the club itself. Her dressing room was small but lovely: Pale blue but with the same feeling of sumptuousness as the rest of the place. She sat down at the makeup table.

"You little piece!"

Elyse looked into the mirror, stupefied. The voice was right, but the language was wrong. Yet, there he was. Nico. She must have misunderstood— She spun around on her chair with a wide grin. "Nico! What a wonderful sur—"

"Cut it cunt." His eyes were as cold as his tone of voice.

Elyse stared at her friend without comprehension. "Nico, what language! What are you doing here in Chicago? Nico, what's happening with you? "

He remained standing only a few feet from her. She had never seen such a look of hatred on his face, except. . .except when he had thrown her Family's true background at her. She felt a shiver in her stomach. Then she saw he was shaking too. She started to stand up, but he pushed her roughly back into the chair.

"No, you'll stay," he ordered through clenched teeth.

"Nico, I wasn't going anywhere. I just—"

"Oh, for God's sake shut up, Bitch. I can't even stand to look at you let alone hear you speak. I don't have the words. I don't even know what to say. There aren't any words filthy enough to describe you."

"Nico, what are you saying, what—"

"Go ahead. Tell me *this* time that you don't know. Like the last time you lied. I believed you then. Maybe I'll be chump enough to believe you again. Go ahead. Tell me more lies!"

"Tell you *what*?" she screamed. "*What*?"

"Tell me you don't know that Lorgan is 'Cantrelli' not 'Cantrell'. Tell me you don't know who owns the casino where you sang in the Bahamas. Tell me you don't know that Lorgan's brother, Carmine, runs gambling junkets there and Lorgan's grandfather, Frankie, Sr., who along with *your* grandfather killed *my* grandfather, and that Frankie, Jr., Lorgan's *father*, is in Washington right now under Senate investigations again. Tell me you don't know this fancy dive you're going to sing in is a front for your half-brother Paulie's drug peddling because New York's still too much under scrutiny for showy things like this by a son of a suspected Boss, and Chicago has always welcomed scum—"Nico's face was white, his eyes full of unshed tears, his voice breaking. "And tell me you don't know I found Lou Roshard this morning in his bed with six bullet holes in his chest. Like cops, Mob hit men always empty their guns. Right?

"Go ahead, *you*, tell me, tell, me, tell me!" He was coming toward her. She shrank back in the chair. He looked as if he would kill her. "I'm in Chicago on a four-hour layover. I'm taking Lou's body to his parents in Denver because *I'm* the one stupid enough to convince him to tell the FBI about your father and Reno becoming his uninvited *business* partners, and I knew about Paulie's new place from sources at home so thought I'd take a look at it during this layover time to see if I could come up with any smart dirt on Paulie. But I find *you* here! So tell me what *you* are doing *here* if not the same as Lou told me you were doing in the Bahamas? But we both know the answer to that, don't we?"

Nico stopped abruptly. He spat at her image in the mirror and holding his hands together as if afraid that parting them would allow him to strangle her, he whirled around, marched out the door and vanished.

Elyse stared at what he had done. She couldn't catch her breath. Nico's saliva was dribbling down the image of her face in the mirror. She raised a hand to her own face, reeling inside from shock and incredulity. She felt the spit there.

FOURTEEN

SHE WANDERED AROUND the club in a daze after Nico left, looking to see if there were any outward signs. None. Normal patrons of the nightclub would never know. Just like the general public never knows about the silent, unwanted partners in many other different types of businesses or the absent forces sitting invisibly at how many Board meetings across the country. Or the money diverted from union pension funds into phony investments, the threats on families of how many business owners if they didn't submit to"going union" by mobster thugs and then forced to provide no-show jobs to lazy gangsters who needed real paychecks to report on their taxes. Or the curtailment of how many investigations into politicians when the answers were found to be too close to home. A drug bar in the back of some nightclub in Chicago—a town famous as the biggest haven for crime and corruption for generations—was small change compared to what went on elsewhere.

Why would her father bother to trick her with such a

devious scheme? Why, when he knew she despised him, would her father do anything to *help* her career? The recording company and now the nightclub? There must be some larger plan at the center of all this. Nico wouldn't lie that Lou Roshard was dead, and she knew now it really had been Paulie's limo this morning. Lorgan? She couldn't bear to think of it. Lorgan's complicity she still didn't know. Nico could be guessing.

It was in the Handicap restroom that she found the door. She tried to imagine where they might think to put the secret entrance to a drug bar. The fake doors in the other bathrooms, like Speakeasy doors? She tried every decorative handle, three in each stall, and they were all fakes. Real doors with real handles, but they didn't open. Then, passing by the separate Handicap bathroom, it dawned on her. On the "fake" door next to the small railing required by law, she heard it—absolutely unnoticeable unless you were listening for it: the click of a working door. Locked but workable. It probably had to be opened from the other side, and she guessed, now, that the little "window" on that particular door was a one-way mirror used for identifying any would-be guest. Originated during Prohibition, when liquor was made illegal by the government, the same procedure was repeating itself, only this time with illegal drugs. How many of the people she sang for would slip through that door?

***

She lay across the bed in their hotel suite. Lorgan would arrive soon. He was already late for lunch. If he was in on this, she would give him a chance to admit it. Could it be possible for him not to know? Or *not* be "Cantrelli"?

She must give him the benefit of the doubt. She remembered all too vividly when Nico had not been as generous to her by hurling the news of her Family at her without any warning. Suddenly, she wished she believed in God. How comforting it would be to think she had someone to pray to that what Nico said wouldn't be true. But this was real life. Either it was true or it wasn't. Period. Out of love, she would set the stage for him to confess. She would make it easy for him by confessing first. She loved Lorgan for what he was now, not what he was forced into by his heritage.

She heard the key card in the lock. Lorgan walked into the room. Seeing her lying on the bed, he rushed over to her. "Darling! Are you all right? Elyse, answer me!"

When she lifted her head, he scooped her into his arms with relief. His concern was real. He held her close, protecting her— She buried her face into his shoulder and sobbed quietly for a long time. He waited silently.

Once she could speak, she sat up and dried her tears with the edge of the bedspread. "Lorgan, I have some things to tell you. I should have told you before, but we were so happy and love was so new to me I didn't want anything unpleasant to mar even one minute of our time together." And if *you* have something to tell *me*, please, *please* do it, her heart begged silently.

She watched his face carefully while she told him everything, starting with Paulie that morning in the limousine. He listened stoically. She told him the identity of her father, how Nico had shocked her about her family with a capitol "F" while they were in college, how her half-sister Claretta confirmed the truth of everything Nico reported, how her mother had known nothing either, how Nico found Lou Roshard murdered this morning, how she found the secret door in the club—

He listened attentively, asking no questions, making no comments, offering no reactions. When she finished, he asked, "Is that all?"

Elyse looked directly into his eyes. "Yes," she lied.

Lorgan paced the room. Should he tell her now? If Nico revealed nothing about his own relationships, Elyse still didn't know. But Nico had suggested at the recording session that his name might really be Cantrelli, a connection easy enough to establish by anyone with reason to snoop, certainly an Internet Blogger. Then Nico *must* know but for some reason chose not to tell Elyse? Why wouldn't he tell her that, too? Maybe he did? Maybe Elyse was testing him? That wasn't like her. She was such a direct person. If she had been told, she would confront him, wouldn't she?

She sat on the bed, waiting. He joined her. "This is a lot you've handed me all at once, darling."

Opening night was one week away. He *must* get her to sing or they'd both be finished. Afterward, he could confess everything and show her the many letters he wrote to her along the way. Then, surely, she would understand he'd been trapped by her father but unexpectedly fell deeply in love with her. They would have time to devise a strategy to get away together because her father would assume things were moving forward as planned and leave them alone for awhile. He couldn't suggest any of these truths or possibilities at *this* fragile point in time or she would refuse to perform in a club associated with her Family, of that he was certain. Zio, Reno, or Paulie were in daily contact with him. He was too much under their eyes to do anything unexpected. Oh, Nico's timing was terrific! He smiled tenderly at the woman who owned his heart so completely.

"As far as the members of your family are concerned, I

don't care who they are. I love you. But these other things, if they are true, are extremely serious. If Lou was killed because he told the authorities your father was muscling in on his recording business, and your father is as top dog in the Mob as you say he is, then the authorities are already riveted on trying to get something solid on your *father*, which has nothing to do *directly* with us because we are under contract with *Lou* for the album, and he's recorded quite a few singers before. Even though he's no longer alive, his reputation is fine. I think it may be in our best interest to go ahead with your opening as if we know nothing of what else is going on at the club. Then, after your two-week gig, we can extricate ourselves naturally without arousing any suspicion and remove ourselves quietly from the picture. Maybe, if your family is who you say they are, just take "Dreamer" and vanish to another life somewhere else. . ."

Elyse watched him carefully, the pain in her head screaming for him to tell her more, screaming there *had* to be more. "But Lorgan, don't you think the coincidence is just too great?" she asked. "My father and two half-brothers involved in both the recording company where I cut my first album and the nightclub where I sing my first professional engagement? It seems to me my father wants me under his thumb all of a sudden. He disowned me for hating his guts when I found out about him. I have disavowed my entire family for several years, contacting not even my dear mother who was as ignorant as I. Now, all of a sudden, he gets involved with my career and tries to help me behind the scenes? Why? What's in it for him to help my career when he knows I despise him and will have nothing to do with him or any of them?" *And how did you really get this gig for me?* she asked herself silently.

"I don't know, Elyse. I'll find out. But, obviously, we must be cautious and not do anything rash to call attention to ourselves. I'll take care of this disturbing development for us. I just don't know how long it will take. Trust me, darling. I love you. I will not let anything or anyone hurt you, not your family, not anyone. Please don't do anything yourself. Just give me time to absorb all this and figure a way out for us *together*. It must be done right. Your family with a capital 'F' obviously doesn't play games. Your half brother must have a legitimate partner because the restaurant owner to whom I sent your demo is okay. He owns several places in Chicago, but this is his first club. That's why I pitched him," he lied.

He got up, deeply preoccupied. "Look, darling. Let me do some exploring into this situation right now. Why don't you get some rest? You must be exhausted. Elyse, look at me. I love you. Trust me. I'll send a lunch tray up for you now, and I'll be back before dinner." He kissed her gently on the forehead and held her head for a long moment between his hands. Then he was gone.

Elyse picked up the phone and dialed the number for Lorgan's personal secretary. "Hello, Lorrie, this is Elyse Gannon. I'm in Chicago and Lorgan mentioned he was going to see Paulie Gadonni, but something must have come up because he's not back yet. I tried his cell, but there's no answer, so I'd like to phone Mr. Gadonni. Do you have the phone number?"

The voice on the other end of the line was officious. "Of course, dear. His number is private, but let me give him a ring and have him call you right back. What's the number of your hotel?"

Elyse laughed into the phone, tears overflowing her cheeks. "Oh, for heaven's sake, here he is right now, coming in the door, so I won't need— Thanks anyway, Lorrie."

She replaced the receiver quickly, trying to contain the sobs being torn from her throat. She gave him his chance, and he lied to her. She was alone now.

FIFTEEN

LORGAN WAITED WITH mounting impatience while the waiter served dinner in the living room of their hotel suite. A great deal of patience had been required of him this past week, and he retained little reserve. He'd tried to reach Nico dozens of times with no success. The young Blogger seemed not to have returned to New York, Lorgan was unable to locate him in Denver where Elyse said Lou Roshard's parents resided, and the kid wasn't answering his cell. He wanted desperately to confirm whether Nico did, in fact, know of his own relationship with the Mob, and if so, how much he knew. Most importantly, if he *did* know, had he told Elyse?

He noted with mounting anxiety her preoccupied withdrawal since she confessed to him—confessed to *him*!—her background, but he reminded himself that such remote behavior could easily be explained away by the understandable pressure of her opening tonight. On the other hand, the preoccupation seemed to carry a taint of distrust? Or, perhaps, his pounding inner turmoil was making him imagine things?

Well the night was here. Last week's rehearsals in California had gone splendidly. She and her group were ready. They would hear the opening chords in three hours. She was ready. So was he.

In two weeks, at the end of her gig at the club, he would take her on another trip, a honeymoon. But *this* honeymoon would also be an escape. They would go abroad and become "lost." He originally considered changing their identities and hiding within the United States. Easy enough to fake identities, but he had been part of Mob life long enough to know that such a plan was virtually impossible, at best short-lived.

If he ever took out insurance on a car, boat, house, or even his own life, there would be applications. Not only did the Mob have hundreds of insurance companies of their own, but they could also get information from other firms by saying he owed back premiums or they were trying to pay him as a beneficiary of someone's will. They would find him.

Their general M.O. would be to first use a connection in the U.S. Social Security office, who could check records for them, and as soon as he used his S.S. number, they would nail him. So he would have to get a fake number, that of someone who died. This was also easy enough, but what about Elyse's career? What about *her* identity?

Plus, if they stayed in the States, they would find him through doctors. Some doctors were always involved with the Mob because they invariably earned money they didn't want to report to the tax boys. They want the money to work for them, however, so in order to keep their holdings from the IRS, they invest it with mobsters to provide money to loan sharks, or to front restaurants or clubs or land, anything to get their under-the-table money invested and returned without Uncle Sam's finding out. Lorgan would no longer be able to frequent any doctor for his allergy pill prescriptions and occasional injections. Plus, as spotty as this medical tax dodging had been in the past, it would undoubtedly increase now with all the new "boutique" and "concierge" doctors trying to get around ever more restrictive government regulations. The whole subject was enough to make him wary.

Oh, yes. Anyone on the inside of *La Cosa Nostra* would find him. And if they found him, they would find her. So he and Elyse could not stay in America. After her gig, they would vanish and go to Europe—Scandinavia—where they might have a chance. He'd get all the fake I.D. needed for both of them. They would go by boat and slip in under the radar of Customs. Because he was a pilot, he could even rent or buy a small plane if need be to move around quickly once in another country. *But he'd have to tell her everything beforehand, including why they had to leave.* She would have to understand that if they married in the U.S., Zio would have succeeded in hooking Elyse back into the Family, and they would be under his thumb forever. But assuming her love could stand the truth once she understood all this, would she go with him even if she still loved him? His mind was a raging battleground: guilt, worry, fear, choices— He forced himself to concentrate on the moment at hand. One step at a time. . .

The waiter poured champagne and left the suite. Lorgan raised his glass. "To Elyse Gannon," he toasted.

Elyse took one sip of her drink to accept his good wishes and then set her glass down. She was to perform in a few hours, so no alcohol and very little food. She had tried again and again—New York, Denver, his cell phone—to reach Nico with no luck. So, she would just have to wait, playing along with Lorgan and her family until she could ask Nico what to do.

Lorgan set a white box on the table containing, she knew, a gardenia for the show. She opened it, ordering herself to be pleased.

But the order was not sufficient to cope with the entire contents of the box. As expected, she found the gardenia nestled as usual into its white tissue paper. But she found something else, too, resting on one of the flower's white petals like a brilliant drop of dew: the large oval of an exquisite, cushion-cut diamond set into a simple gold band. Elyse kept her eyes on the gift, fighting conflicting emotions. She knew that the pleasure showing on her face was at the same time clouded with distrust. She tried to hide the distrust.

Lorgan rose and coming around to her side placed his hands gently on her shoulders. "An opening night wish for success, darling. . ." he hesitated, turning her around to face him. "And a promise to love you forever as Mrs. Cantrell, if you will."

She couldn't contain it then. The emotional impact was too much. The rush of truth too great, rising in her like a torrent to refute his lie. "You mean Mrs. Cantrelli, don't' you? Did my father order you to marry me as well as manage my career?"

Lorgan answered quickly and openly. *This* was the time? Just before her opening night? But he had no choice now. He had to tell her. "Yes, Elyse, he did."

***

She sat at her dressing room table applying makeup. As she moved her hands, the diamond on her finger sparkled in the mirror. Her heart soared and then sank between joy and pain.

He had confessed it all to her. The other side of the coin she revealed to him a week ago. He denied nothing and elaborated everything. She believed he told her the truth. There were no more secrets, now, concerning their past. She believed, too, that he honestly did love her. And she knew that, despite everything, she still loved him, loved the real man buried beneath the man he was forced to be by circumstance of birth. She had forgiven him. No man should ever be put in the position into which Lorgan was ordered by her father, and going back over his initial coldness toward her, she also believed he had not planned and actually resisted their love affair. She blotted away a tear that threatened to smudge her mascara.

He suggested fleeing right after her gig. He even suggested that if they married and stayed in the States, Zio might be satisfied that his diabolical plan had succeeded and leave them alone until he could mount her career and hopefully gain a celebrity status that would make it impossible for her father to control them further. But she knew that none of this was possible. It was too late for love to save them no matter what they did, because she could never know what other secrets Lorgan might keep in the future even if they were married. She could never trust him again. He lied to her once and had been very successful at the lying. He could do it again. She would never have any way of knowing what else her father might order Lorgan to do, holding her as hostage. Lorgan might not want to follow her father's orders—he hadn't wanted to this time—but she knew he would if either his own or her life was at stake. Zio would never leave them alone, and if they had a child, he could hold that child as hostage; therefore, she could never know the real motivation behind anything Lorgan might do. No love could survive that kind of existence. Their births were their curses for life.

She made a call on her cell phone.

Getting into her gown, she forced herself to put all thoughts aside until her debut was over. She looked at herself in the full-length mirror. The gown Lorgan had chosen was clasped high around her throat by a circle of rhinestones, the rest of it cascading in soft folds of nearly transparent white chiffon to the floor, the stones sparkling as they scattered down the front of the gown like an effervescent Milky Way. Her shoulders and arms were bare, their only ornament being another narrower circle of stones on each wrist, catching a wisp of fabric on either side and lifting it to give the faint suggestion of wings when she raised her arms during a song. Her hands, too, were unadorned except for the diamond solitaire. She decided to keep the ring and wear it for the same reason she decided to perform her opening night: In tribute to what could have been. Because she intended to be happy tonight, as she should have been.

Her long hair was swept up and away from her face into a sophisticated twist by another, tinier band of stones for this glamorous debut, but at the opening chord of her last song she would pull one large hairpin from the center of the chignon, and the tumble of burnished copper would fall loosely around her shoulders and surround her face for a most sensuous finale. She was the sun. The stars of light embedded into the deep blue background of the club would become her setting: the sky at dusk. Lorgan had choreographed it all. With the subtle use of lighting, he would guide her audience through a musical night from sunset, through the dark, and finally into the burst of a sunrise released by her pulsing music and the tumbling cascade of her hair. He always insisted on ending with the beginning, and after the dramatic finale, leaving everyone in soft, pastel pink light, her audience, her musicians, herself (and him most of all, she suspected) with the quiet promise of a new day. It was an obsession with him, to transform her from a sunset to a sunrise.

He walked into her dressing room, then, looking as if the promise was already fulfilled. He told her the truth, and she forgave him. After this two week stretch of performing, he would take her far away to a new life for both of them, far and safe from any harm. He lifted her hand and pressed his lips to the ring. "Sing to me, darling," he whispered. Then, handing the gardenia to her, he led her down a small hallway into the entrance wing of the stage. Leaving her alone to prepare herself mentally, he took his seat near the stage to fight back happy tears as he heard her introduction.

"Ladies and gentlemen, Elyse Gannon!"

She didn't look into the crowd as she floated exultantly onto the stage. She didn't care who was there. For this one night they all belonged, whoever they were. Sitting on Lorgan's or *her* piano—did it matter?—she let Milo's horn lead her unresistingly into the dark, and then, commanding her right, she shattered the night with her sound. She was a force of life. She was its meaning. She was tender, she was haunting. She was light and energy and speed. She was playful, she was teasing, she was seductive. She was purpose. She was time. She was love. She was woman. All these belonged to her. She took them one song after another and offered them to everyone who had the ears to hear, the eyes to see, the minds to know.

At the end of her performance, Lorgan rose to his feet along with the rest of the audience. Everyone was applauding. He was standing with her future, her listeners. They loved her. Perhaps she *would* rise so fast to the top of celebrity that her father couldn't reach her after all? Perhaps if her name became famous enough fast enough, they wouldn't have to leave? He caught the gardenia, kissed it, tossed it joyfully back to her, and rose to rush backstage and be there when she finished her encore, which was definitely going to be demanded by this enthusiastic audience.

Glowing with happiness at the crowd's applause, Elyse sailed from the stage on the jubilant path of her triumph. Picking up a small overnight bag waiting behind one of the curtains, she then turned and ran out the stage door of the club.

Lorgan arrived backstage amid the excited din of the audience calling for an encore just in time to see the door slam shut. He reached the sidewalk only in time to note the license plate of a limousine as it sped away from the curb.

SIXTEEN

THE OPAQUE WINDOW on the door of his office was broken, but oddly, newspaper sheets were taped over the hole from the inside. The door itself was still secured but could have been opened by someone breaking the window, reaching in, and unlocking the door to get into the room and then re-locking it behind them. Nico used his key and opened the door slowly. The office was undisturbed. Strange. He placed his bags near the desk—he had come directly from the airport—and walked carefully into the bathroom.

He saw her immediately. Standing above him, one foot on the sink, one on the toilet, a letter opener raised in her hand, the look of a wild animal in her eyes. Then she was on top of him, the letter opener clattering to the tile, knocking them both to the floor, clutching him and crying.

"Oh, Nico, thank heavens you're here. I've been trying to reach you for over a week, but even your cell phone wasn't answering. Nico, you've got to help me, tell me where I can go to tell everything I know, Nico—"

"Okay. Okay. Quiet now. I'll take care of you. I was in Denver with Lou's parents and wanted to talk to no one else. It's my fault he's dead because I convinced him to go to the Feds. I'm having a very hard time living with that. Shhh. . . Quiet down and tell me what has happened."

She was still crying uncontrollably. "I took a limousine to the airport in Chicago immediately after opening night at the club and changed out of my evening gown in the Ladies' Room. When I got to New York, I took a cab from JFK to Grand Central Station, then a subway up to 125th Street before taking another cab here. I don't think anybody followed me, but I mixed up the route just in case Lorgan alerted someone here to track me down or came to New York himself to try and find me because he knows I've run away. I left the club before an encore! He knows you're the one who told me about the club, so he may find out where you live and go to your apartment building to try and see you, but I don't think he can find out about your little office space way up in this warehouse building for your 'Family' investigations, so that's why I came here. If he finds me, he won't let me do what I want to do. Nico! We have to get me some place where *nobody* can find me! My father must have heard from Paulie that I ran away from the club, so he may be looking for me too. I'm so afraid of him. That's why I hid here in your bathroom."

"Elyse, please! Try to calm down." He could feel her shaking in his arms. This was no act. She was terrified to the core. If Lorgan or, worse, Zio really were in pursuit, there was no time— He pulled himself away from her and slapped her face.

Elyse stopped crying instantly and stared at him in horror, mystified and hurt.

Nico took her tear-stained face in his hands. "I'm sorry,

but you have to get hold of yourself. Now, why are you here, who exactly have you run away from, and what is it you want to do?"

"You were right. Everything you said in my dressing room, about Lorgan and Paulie, about everything." She was speaking brokenly but quietly now, "Nico, you must believe me. *I didn't know!* But I do now, and. . . *and it has to stop!* You know more about my father's activities than I do, so tell me things I can tell anybody, the police or whomever, that I might know having grown up in his house, which could substantiate what *you* know about but may lack corroboration. If you tell me what to remember, I must be able to help—"

She stopped, suddenly back in control of herself, as purpose reasserted itself in her mind. "Nico, my father and all of his kind are not some glamorized gangster movie. They are real. They're evil. I want to be the one to give whatever information is required to see that my father spends the rest of his life behind bars."

"And Lorgan?" Nico asked slowly, noticing the diamond ring on her left hand.

Elyse fought back more tears. "I love him," she choked. "But the only way to free him is to leave him. I figured it out once he told me my father ordered him to manage my career and entice me to marry him. My father never wanted Lorgan as Boss, but he's in line. Without me—*a Gadonni*—as Lorgan's wife, Zio knows Lorgan isn't strong enough to head the California Family. And you can believe this or not, Nico, but Lorgan never wanted any part of it. He didn't plan on actually falling in love with me. He tried to avoid it! But it happened, and we do love each other. He wants out. He never *wanted* to be in, but he was *born* in just like I was. He thinks we can get away from all of them. But I don't want to get away now, even if we could. My father has done everything he could to ruin my life, even rig things to help my *career* in phony ways to tie me to the Family. That Scum Bastard choreographed my career *and* my love! Now I will not rest until I've done everything I can to ruin *his* life.

"Nico!" Elyse scrambled up from the floor, pulling him up as well. "You must have a recorder here in the office. Get it quickly, and I'll give you answers to any questions you can think of. Then, no matter what happens, you'll have a permanent record. I can give you the names of judges and politicians and socialites and entertainers and businessmen who came to my father's breakfasts when I was young. My mother and I were always so proud he was such an important businessman to have those prominent people come over like that.

"Oh, Nico, they're the guilty ones, dealing voluntarily with Mob animals, giving them legitimacy, using them to gain power of their own or getting some sick little thrill by hobnobbing with people who violate the law beyond any boundaries of civility. They should feel revulsion, not intrigue! Don't they realize that people like my father are not just law-breakers but they kill *innocent* people too, not just each other like in the movies but ruining the lives of *anyone* who gets in their way or has something they want? What's the matter with people in this country, who behave as if *La Cosa Nostra* members are romantic Hollywood characters? They're real, they're vile, and they couldn't exist in organized form without acceptance by those other people outside the Mob. Let me give you the names of some of those people!"

Nico pushed her disheveled hair gently away from her face. He would never doubt her again. She really never had known of any of it. He was incredibly wrong to hurt her so.

"When did you get here?" he asked softly.

"Night before last. Poor Lorgan. He must be so worried, so confused— But I couldn't tell him ahead of time. He wouldn't have let me go—"

"Your father must be looking for you because Paulie for sure reported to him. He knows how strong headed you can be. Look at the trouble you caused the last time you found out about him. Your mother's love for your father turned to hate, too, after Claretta confirmed the truth. I know. I've heard."

Elyse was somber, thinking. "Maybe Lorgan told my father that my leaving him was some personal problem between us."

"You've been missing for almost two days. I better call one of my Washington contacts and ask him what to do with you. But I don't think I can stand by and let you put yourself in danger. I already failed with Lou, and I can't have two deaths on my conscience. Have you eaten?"

"No, but I don't care about that. Nico, even if we go to Washington, I want you to bring the recorder. Then I can tell you all I know on the plane, and even if they get me at some point, you'll still have that. Wait! Better yet. *You* tell *me* everything *you* know. I mean about Reno and all the rest of the *next-in-line* leaders all over the country too. Maybe I can break apart the whole dynasty. Lorgan said the reason my father needs to solidify his power by "marrying" the east and west coasts is because that FBI raid a few years ago caused so much mayhem within the ranks he's still having difficulty maintaining absolute control. So if the Mob is already jumbled internally, maybe I can mess it up even more and my information could foment a really big war where they all will finally destroy each other. At least, if I give calculated info to set them against each other, the *national* web of syndicate ties may come unraveled. What do you think? You've been collecting dirt for years and disseminating it as best you can little by little. So let me do the dirty work big time. The Boss of all Boss's *daughter*— That should cause an earthquake or two!"

"I don't know. Once you spill to the FBI, if the Senate wants you to testify and you go public, your life will not exist after that Elyse. You must know this."

"I don't care. I really don't. I really don't! I really don't! *He ruined both my love and my career*! There's nothing left for me anyway. . ."

Nico wrapped his dearest friend into his arms and held her close until she stopped sobbing and looked up at him with the serene smile he knew so well when she made up her mind on any subject in the world. Nothing would stop her mission now—

SEVENTEEN

LORGAN WATCHED HIS father take the Fifth over and over again on TV. It was the tenth appearance he'd made before the Senate's investigation committee on organized crime over the past thirty-eight months. At virtually every question, he merely reiterated the same monotonous words: "I refuse to answer on the grounds it might incriminate me."

He looked around at Elyse's—Elena's—Family as they nodded and joked in approval of their friend. Mobsters always liked to see themselves in newspapers and on TV. They couldn't resist because their egotistical desire for celebrity was so great that even though they were labeled "crime" figures, no one could ignore the fact that they were given the same cover-story status as presidents and royalty. They were just as newsworthy in American society. It never occurred to them that celebrity and famous were different from notoriety and infamous because the press didn't know the difference anymore, and the American public's insatiable thirst for sensationalism made so little distinction between heroes and statesmen versus gangsters and politicians that the "crime" label didn't resonate any longer. There was even a Mafia Museum in Vegas that tracked their history with newspaper articles, photos, and memorabilia. Even though the Mob lost its serious power to the Disney-type hotels there twenty-five years ago, they loved that museum, where jerks went every day and paid money to get a gander at their mug shots.

Lorgan felt sick to his stomach. How he *despised* these people. But at last he no longer feared them. He was here in Zio's house, true, but not just because of the "come in" invitation to grill him about her disappearance. The invitation-command had been given, of course, but he'd responded willingly because he couldn't find her either and hoped he might discover some clues from Zio so he could get to her first. How she had hurt him! She didn't trust him after all. But then why did she accept his engagement ring? Why throw the gardenia to him at the close of her show? Why? *Why?* There were so many unanswered questions. She was complicating matters terribly. What drove her to do this?

He'd searched everywhere he could think of: his own Malibu home and both Milo's and Nico's New York apartments, easily breaking in to both with a credit card and leaving no trace. Zio was looking for her too, but she had eluded them all. Lorgan knew she went first to New York because the limousine service had a record of the car that took her to O'Hare and to which terminal she was left off. He'd convinced the airline to confirm her name on their passenger list, so it must have been from New York that she flew on to D.C., where through Frankie's connections Zio learned she intended to testify voluntarily. Lorgan shook his head in despair. She was making it very difficult for him to help either of them now.

Elyse's half-brother Reno was laughing at the TV. "See how good he looks, Lorgan. I don't care where he is, newspapers, TV, even mug shots. Your old man always looks so damned good."

It was true, Lorgan thought. Frankie Cantrelli was handsome in ways both strong and silent. He had soft brown eyes and a benign expression that was evident even in photographs taken by the police. "Never let anyone know how you feel," his father always warned him. Until Elyse came into his life, Lorgan had followed his advice.

Unlike Elyse, he always knew his father was part of the Mob. On 116th Street, no male kid from kindergarten on needed to be told that New York was a sanctuary and playground of La *Cosa Nostra*. Democrats, Republicans, and La *Cosa Nostra*. Unlike love and marriage, which could be separated, political figures and Mob leaders were a faithful match. Nobody thought for one second you could have one without the other. That had changed dramatically over the past few decades because La *Cosa Nostra* had purposefully gone underground to stay out of the public eye, but the connections still existed, mostly in the boroughs. So Mob members got a laugh out of certain politicians investigating Mob leaders. The irony of it all was worth a good laugh.

Lorgan's father taught him many things. Even now, so many years beyond his youth with no need to do so, when driving at night on any road or highway, he was aware of every car behind him. Whenever he passed another car, he observed its body style and State license plate and tried to get a quick look at the driver. By habit, he also found his alertness intensify whenever a car behind him speeded up to pass him. He studied road maps carefully before any trip, automatically noting exits, detours and possible escape routes. None of this was necessary, but the habits were drilled into him when he was young. Habits hard to shake.

Frankie taught his son about the special use of pay phone booths even earlier in his youth by calling the nine-year-old boy at home and making folksy conversation in Sicilian before slipping in two numbers, the first identifying the locale of the phone booth where Lorgan was to go and the second dictating the time at which he was to appear. Then just before the appointed time, Lorgan would bike his way to the designated phone booth, where Frankie would call him and they could speak freely without worry of the home phone being tapped. Sometimes Frankie gave Lorgan a small message to deliver, but mostly it was a teaching exercise, the only kind of father-son relationship Lorgan ever knew.

What a family education! To this day—long after the regular use of cell phones and iPads—he still kept tubes of dimes and quarters in his own home, pretending they were for the jukebox, which in fact they were. But that wasn't the only reason. The tubes of coins were another habit learned while very young. To this day, even though phone booths were practically nonexistent anywhere, he still felt suffocated by emotional fear in any small space even resembling one, and that included the dreaded church confessional, where as a young boy he also waited through fretful moments before the stern priest slapped open the sliding screen to learn of Lorgan's transgressions against God.

Guns he never could learn. He remembered when, as a boy of ten, he waited long hours on the sidewalk with Tony Pedino for Tony's father to return from a meeting with the local padrone. Mr. Pedino had recently gone into the olive oil business with a Tuscan company and was doing rather well. Too well, according to the Mob leader, who also owned a competitive olive oil company in Tuscany. Tony's father had been warned once before to get out of that region of Italy. But he hadn't obeyed. The next thing Lorgan knew, he was attending Mr. Pedino's funeral with Tony. And the man everybody knew shot Tony's father had the gall to send a big blanket of red roses to cover the casket. Lorgan would never forget how eleven-year-old Tony had dived into the flowers, tearing them off the coffin and throwing them wildly in the faces of his father's mourners.

No, Lorgan had never been able to learn guns, at least in the way *his* Family used them. *Possession* of arms he could understand. It was in the Second Amendment of the Constitution, after all, for the protection of law abiding citizens against the likes of his Family, and—in the end— their own potentially oppressive government. But the other? No matter how many gun control laws were leveled at the general populace, *criminals* will get guns here, there and everywhere. Period. How well he had observed and learned—

Then, later, it suddenly hadn't mattered. By a stroke of luck, he began to be considered Jewish. His own mother was Jewish by birth, but that was of no technical import because he was the *son* of an *Italian man*. Nevertheless, one day when he was in high school, a big mobster came into the men's store where he worked part time to make extra pocket money. After watching Lorgan politely and meticulously wrap up his selections because his regular, cocky salesman was out to lunch, he tossed a fifty-dollar bill onto the counter. Lorgan gave the tip to the outraged clerk when he returned from his break, but from that day forward the mobster always asked for "Lorgan, that nice Jewish kid," which drove the other clerk and his own father crazy but which in some strange way took the pressure off him to follow his father's footsteps precisely. After all, with his mother being Jewish, if her son had a first name like "Lorgan" and seemed to appear Jewish to certain Italians, then even his own father could accept that he was at least "different" and could be given some leeway. It might explain why his eldest son was too weak to kill someone — anyone — to become a *made member*, didn't want a gun of his own even for protection, and went into a frivolous thing like show business —

The two groups had always worked in surprising harmony, however, the Italians respecting the Jews for their financial brains, and the Jews preferring to stay quietly behind the scenes and let the Italians use "muscle" when needed. In his grandfather's time, Jewish mobsters were actually called the "Kosher Nostra," hanging out in Manhattan's Lower East Side delis and introducing money-oriented things like loan sharking and illegal gambling to the world of organized crime. But even though they might work well together — still today — they were startling different in temperament. So once Frankie was convinced that his first son's Jewish heritage was so obvious as to make a Mob chieftain notice, he left Lorgan largely alone and concentrated on his younger son, Carmine, instead. None of this mattered to *Zio* one bit, of course, who still viewed Lorgan as the heir apparent to his father's position as *Boss* in California simply because whatever else he wasn't, he was still the eldest son. Primogeniture held fast above all else in Zio's ossified mind.

Suddenly, Lorgan gripped the arm of his chair. Elyse's beautiful face had appeared on the TV screen.

"Never let anyone know how you feel," his father had lectured. Sitting in the middle of his loved-one's hostile family, now, Lorgan hoped to God that he'd learned the lesson well enough to get through what was coming his way.

No one in Mob history had ever snitched *voluntarily* at any of the government's crime hearings. And a *woman* at that! Unprecedented. Mob members, who "turned" did it out of necessity in return for the safety provided by the Feds afterward from other mobsters, who were already out for their heads or to shorten or eliminate their own jail sentences. Lorgan looked around the room cautiously. No nods of approval now, no jokes, no laughs. The "Elder Statesman" crime Boss's *daughter*—his own flesh and blood—*for no gain on her own part*! This was a phenomenon new to all of them, including Lorgan, who sat stunned at what Elyse had chosen to do. Zio looked daggers at Doria, as if she were somehow to blame for their daughter's behavior. Doria remained expressionless in her corner rocking chair.

Elyse began by explaining her father's use of scams, speaking calmly into the microphone, into the ears of millions of viewers all over the country. "One of my father's favorite means of driving a legitimate company into bankruptcy is the three-step-scam. "Elyse felt as composed as she looked. This was her moment to say "No" to all her father had done to "help" her career and to say *"No more"* to the man she dearly loved. Finally it was also her chance to say "No" to all of *La Cosa Nostra* members and their supporters, who although more subtle in their dealings today than in their notorious past still festered like a feudal sore in America, continuing old ways and old wars that were at first incongruent with the promise of a new country but later incorporated into America's own growing brand of "respectable" crony capitalism. She hoped her father was watching her on TV at this moment. *This is for you, Zio,* she thought. *I hope to hell it hangs you.*

"First, the Mob forms a corporation fronted by a man who has a clean record. That doesn't mean he's not a crook, it just means he's never been caught. He's called a 'pencil'. Then a large deposit is made into a bank in order to establish credit. This is called 'nut money,' and it will eventually be withdrawn.

"The corporation rents offices, staffs them, and orders merchandise from as many *legitimate* companies as possible. The larger the orders the better because the *Mob's* company appears more legitimate that way. The initial orders are placed the first month and paid for in full. Then during the second month even larger orders are placed and only one-quarter of the amount due is paid. The third month is saved for the really big orders, when the credit built up during the preceding months can be used, and goods like jewelry, appliances, and computer equipment make up a large portion of the orders because they can be turned into cash quickly.

"After this three-month period, no more money is paid out and the merchandise is converted to cash through a 'fence' or a Mob surplus property agent who has enough inventory to mix in 'scam' goods without detection. Some of the legitimate companies, who originally supplied the goods, are forced into bankruptcy by their creditors because they have never been paid themselves for all the goods that were purchased by the Mob company, so how could they pay their creditors? The legitimate companies' assets not already appropriated by the scam operators are then liquidated to pay their legitimate creditors as best they can. Very often the lawful companies never realize what hit them. It all happens so fast and so 'normally'."

Worried to the core by her words, Lorgan felt certain she must have been tutored by Nico. She could have no first-hand knowledge of anything she related. But since her family couldn't imagine how she got her information, they stared in shocked stupor at her astounding accuracy.

Elyse was cool as a cucumber. "Another type of scamming practiced by *La Cosa Nostra* is to force itself into one point of a legitimate chain of operation. No business operates alone. Every concern has suppliers to buy from and customers to sell to. So when a Mob company introduces itself anywhere along that line it affects all of the businesses involved. For example, New Yorkers pay a few cents a pound in '*Cosa Nostra* tax' for all beef sold in Manhattan and the boroughs because most of the meat coming there from midwest slaughter houses passes through two middlemen instead of the usual one. These additional meat brokers are *Cosa Nostra* men. My cousin Joe Tattalo is one. The prices they charge are eight to twelve cents higher than the price of honest brokers, which averages out to at least a ten-cent *per pound* increase on all meat purchased by consumers. This may not sound like much, but do the math and see how it adds up for all meat purchases for one year. It's especially when the Mob can establish conduits like this, completely tying up a certain aspect of an otherwise legitimate business that the public suffers, because there's no choice. If you want meat, you have to pay the price because the Mob is embedded forcefully into a chain in which the customer is always the last link.

"And don't forget the Mob's activity within different labor unions all over the country. One New York Family, alone, has for decades controlled the Cement and Concrete Union Local 6A. Another Family does such a bizarre thing as extorting members of the International Longshoremen's Association to force the workers to give a portion of their annual *Christmas royalty payments* to the Mob as sort of a 'tax.' Organized crime's corrupt influence in the ports is pervasive, and the unions don't do a thing to protect the workers because the union leaders are in bed with the Mob— Remember a few months ago when back-page news reported a federal racketeering indictment connecting the garbage-hauling industry of New York City to extortion of Mob figures or crews? The underground plague is everywhere."

Lorgan felt Zio's burning black eyes coming to rest on him more and more often as his daughter talked. Finally, his voice low with rage, he asked, "I wonder where Elena learned all this technical stuff, Lorgan. Not from her father. She never knew until some years back about my 'business' and even then never in detail. Why is she doing this? I see a rock on her finger, which should mean things are proceeding smoothly. So why is she doing this, and where did she learn all this shit? She knows a lot from girlhood, but not this much. Maybe you and she have other plans of your own now? Maybe she learned these details from a future husband, who has something like a conscience to cool?"

Lorgan didn't answer. He, too, noticed Elyse was wearing his diamond engagement ring while she testified. What this really meant, he couldn't guess. But he began to understand the incongruity of wearing it at the same time she testified. She was probably wearing it as a silent signal of love to him without realizing that it connected him directly with her defiant act against her father and the Mob, which could look like nothing but a conspiracy to others.

Suddenly the doorbell rang. Zio sent one of his thugs to

unlock and answer it. "Dumdum!" the man greeted her, surprised. "I don't think The Old Man wants to see you so soon."

Zio's oldest daughter pushed angrily past him and flopped down onto a chair. "I need help, God damn it, Zio. The Feds are sitting on her closer than a stripe on a skunk. Give me Louie and Joey, three no serial-numbered vehicles installed with CB radios—we can't use cell phones—and we'll drive the new cars back right away. With the CBs, three of us can take turns following her, so it won't look suspicious and keep us in contact with each other at the same time."

No one in the room turned their eyes from the TV because everyone in the room already knew what Claretta was talking about. Except for two. Two who did not realize that the Hit order had already been given. This was an unexpected and highly unusual piece of news. It wasn't just that Zio ordered one daughter to kill another one, which was shocking enough, but also because a Boss rarely gave such orders personally—they were given by the Underboss—so for Zio to give the Hit order directly carried powerful weight for the deed to be done and done quickly, with no excuses. His young daughter must die for her treason, and his older daughter had been put in quite a spot. Zio must trust her above all others because if, as a Hit person designated from the top, she failed to kill her mark, she might well be next.

This mind-jolting information caused a quick eye exchange between Doria and Lorgan that went unnoticed by the others because it was so fast, so automatic. The mother loved Elena, her only child. The fiancé loved Elyse, the woman he wanted to love and live with for the rest of his life. Neither of them knew how or where or when, but

ALEXANDRA YORK

Lorgan and Doria understood without a word spoken that they had just sealed a silent, sacred pact together to try to save their beloved.

126

EIGHTEEN

BECAUSE OF NERVOUSNESS, Doria had trouble inserting the cassette into the slot of the old machine and pushing the right buttons. The last time she looked at the wedding video was five long years ago, when Elena uprooted her whole existence with accusations toward her husband that would change her own life forever. A wife deceived. A mother forbidden to see her only child. A woman who began to suspect for the first time that somewhere along life's path, she should have taken some responsibility for herself, for her ignorance, for the passive acceptance of her narrow existence. She realized way too late that from girlhood on the realities of life were not hers to know. When only seven and sent to the convent school, she was fated to grow up in a state of grace and innocence and to learn about God and God's ways from cloistered nuns. About man or the real world, she never learned at all.

She remembered loving the convent, though, its tranquility and its uncomplicated atmosphere of simple obedience. It had been with great reluctance—with fear, even—that she boarded the plane after graduation and headed for America to live with an aunt and uncle because her parents felt that a better marriage could be arranged. She could still picture her parents standing in the airline terminal, weeping together over the loss of "God's child," as they called her, but believing, too, that their sheltered daughter's life would be easier with an American husband.

Thankfully, her aunt and uncle had gathered her to their family's bosom as if she *were* a child of God himself. She didn't realize that they found her docile temperament a joyous change from their own boisterous kids. She found her new life so exciting that she thrilled in every little experience, like riding in the front car of a subway or drinking a Coke.

She never knew it was her quiet politeness and her childish, delightful receptiveness to her new American life that drew the recently widowed Rinaldo Gadonni to her, the kind of girl mobsters commonly referred to as "forbidden fruit." Or that his deceased wife, Sicilian in looks and nature, had been coarse and loud and demanding like most of the other neighborhood women, sitting long summer afternoons on the stoops of their apartment buildings, gossiping with each other and screaming at their children. Or that she floated conspicuously among those southern Italian women like a clean, innocent, northern breeze blown sweetly into their midst from far away across the sea.

How could she have known that let alone being a mobster himself, her future husband kept a mistress when he first met her or that he was so taken by *her* "forbidden fruit" that he ousted his own *gumar* immediately and courted her in celibacy for two full years, patiently gaining her trust and transferring her obedience to God into obedience to him.

Doria forced her hands to stop trembling as she struggled with the unfamiliar machine. And *she* had let her dependence on her husband happen. It seemed so natural to come from an austere Italian Catholic convent to the bed of a much older, handsome, wealthy, magnetic man, who introduced her to a life full of pleasures. She had been surprised at her slowly growing romantic attraction to a man the age of her father, but perhaps that's why she trusted him so completely. Before Rinaldo, she never thought about sexual pleasure, but he made her feel as safe and protected within the walls of his home as she ever felt within the confines of God's house, so she learned to rely on him and learn from him and, eventually, love making love with him. She felt comfortable with the rules. She did not have to make any decisions as the wife of this strong, Italian-American man. There were no questions to be asked, no paths to be defined— It was all there: her days planned for her, her future guaranteed with no requirements on her part other than to obey. Rinaldo took care of her in every way. She had no responsibilities, and she loved her husband for all the new and thrilling experiences during their years together: the move from his apartment to a beautiful, spacious home on Long Island, the parties, the jewels, the furs, the opera, museums, friends, even the joyful pain of childbirth and motherhood, never suspecting, never wondering. . .because he was both husband and father to her.

Until Elena's outburst, she never wandered or wondered beyond the comfortable cocoon that Rinaldo spun around her. But to do something on her own impetus, she was helpless. She knew that now. She couldn't even run a simple video machine even though she'd seen it operated by her husband dozens of times and managed it once before by herself right after Elena repudiated her family. It seemed she could do nothing by herself, but now she knew she would have to do a great deal in order to save her child's life.

Nothing in her past had prepared her for this day. It never occurred to her that in return for her security, she had given up her Will. First to God. Then to Rinaldo. She could have asked Rinaldo to wait until she read the newspapers before he left them with holes after cutting out whole sections he needed for himself for some reason. She could have watched her own favorite programs on one of the color TV sets in the house. She could have requested their lives be private at least once in awhile and asked Rinaldo to cut down the regularity of his men-friend visits. She could have. But she never did. Now, she *would* find the strength to do what she should do for the first time in her forty-seven years—

She'd wrapped the tiny note—"Wedding pictures?"— into Lorgan's napkin yesterday morning before placing it beside his breakfast plate and staring at him intently for one brief second in the hope he would understand the importance of the napkin. Her hand did not shake then, but relief spread through her like an ache when, understanding the warning in her eyes, Lorgan carefully placed the napkin in his lap without opening it right away. This morning, inside the bag with pork bread, she found detailed instructions, including where to find the airport limo at the shopping center, a plane ticket, and a bottle of pills. She remembered with fondness how, when both of them were in their teens, Lorgan began bringing her the freshly baked rolls. Today that same boy, a man now, was helping her save her daughter from her husband.

Doria relaxed back in her chair at last. The video was finally in place and the right buttons pushed, revealing the filmed recording of her marriage to Rinaldo for the last time. . .for her. But now she was going to watch it neither to identify the gangsters attending nor out of resentment at the lie perpetrated against her but out of some bewildering need to view the possibilities of such a day, the promise of that day, the future that could have been, might have been—

For the very first time, she noticed the remarkable resemblance between herself at that young age and Elena now. Her own long, naturally reddish-tinged hair, sparkled with her favorite flowers of daisies on her wedding day, Rinaldo having arranged for thousands of them flown in from California because they were out of season in New York to adorn the tables and float from the ceiling while taking their vows.

She could taste again the sour bubbles of her first champagne as she and Rinaldo and over eight-hundred guests drank a truckload of it, a wedding gift from some distributor. She listened again to the rich, romantic sounds of the large orchestra that played for dancing in the ballroom of the old Plaza Hotel. She watched in wonder, now, as prominent politicians, priests, businessmen, entertainers, and wealthy socialites mingled in complete harmony with other guests whom she now knew to be the top men of the underworld.

She also observed the way those men dressed then, realizing that their rank within the organization could be determined by their clothing: the lower-echelon men in white dinner jackets, while the mid-level Lieutenants wore light blue. The Captains all dressed in black tuxedos, and along with the principal males in the wedding party, the

Bosses wore formal cutaways.

After the reception, during which Rinaldo bragged to her about receiving over half-a-million dollars in cash as wedding gifts, they flew to Europe for a honeymoon: Rome and Florence first, and finally ending their trip at the small village in the North, where she had beamed with pride as her new husband hosted a magnificent party for the whole town in her parents' honor. She remembered feeling like Cinderella that wonderful day.

It had all been so beautiful and so promising. Perhaps that's why she felt this last, irresistible compulsion to re-live it once more. The next eyes to view this video would see none of the beauty, she knew. They would be counting heads and matching faces.

Well so be it. The wedding? Her whole life? Nothing but a dream. Her hands steady with purpose now, Doria removed the video without difficulty and inserted it decisively into its plastic jacket. She placed it in a shopping bag alongside the wedding album of still photos and covered both items with soiled clothes for the cleaners. She walked resolutely out the front door, past Rinaldo's body guard, out of the dream and into the clear light of reality.

NINETEEN

A FEW SENATORS SQUIRMED in their chairs. For some reason, this young woman made them feel as if they were under investigation as well as the criminal organization against which she was there to testify. She was a rare and beautiful plum to present to the TV public—the voters— offering this inside peek at the underworld as the *daughter* of Rinaldo "Zio" Gadonni, the Prime Minister of crime. About this they were elated. On the other hand, certain of them felt an inner uneasiness, a suspicion made up only of vibrations, perhaps, but still a suspicion that this girl held men such as they somehow responsible for making Mob activities possible in the first place. It was the way she put things. She almost made it sound as if nearly everything she revealed about *La Cosa Nostra* could have flourished only in soil plowed by the government.

Just moments ago, she seemed to indicate that the various, individual crime gangs would never have become organized at all by her grandfather were it not for the enormous undertaking of supplying an entire nation with liquor during Prohibition, a condition enacted by the government that gave the "Families" their real start. Even now, as she explained the Mob's infiltration into legitimate businesses, they got weird reverberations spinning around in their heads as they listened.

"My father had two very good reasons, actually, for leading racketeers into the legitimate business world, altering the successful but brutal Prohibition-inspired organization instituted by my grandfather and bringing things up to date with more subtle, modern activities. First, they would be able to show a legitimate income on which legitimate taxes would be paid in order to circumvent the fate of Al Capone and others of that previous generation, who were imprisoned on tax evasion convictions. That way, they could continue their newly gained bootlegging monopoly long after repeal through hidden control of some of the then-legalized *legitimate* brewers, distillers, and distributers of liquor and beer. Once the Mob became familiar with the normal intricacies of straight business in a straight society, they saw that their horizons in legal ventures were unlimited because they would always have the edge over law-abiding businessmen. By inserting their own brand of tactics, including fraud, blackmail, corruption, and extortion into the business world, it was fairly easy to outsmart law-abiding businessmen, who most of the time never knew what happened until it was too late."

The Senator from New York interrupted her. "Ms. Gadonni, if you don't mind, we're actually more interested in *concrete examples* of present-day Mob activity, similar to the scams you already talked about." This particular Senator was well aware that the former Attorney General and now Governor of his fine state was heavily involved in prostitution racketeering and had, in his previous position, indicted the leaders of certain Mob prostitute rings in order to eliminate competition.

***

Claretta switched the control of her CB radio to channel 33. Shit, these things had been out of date for so long, she'd forgotten how to use them. But today, these specially installed devices were important, so she calmed herself to the task in front of her. "Louie? Joey? You there?"

Joey's voice was first. "Here." Then Louis. "I got it."

"Okay. Now once she leaves the building and while we're tailing her, stay no more than one mile apart and keep in touch. I'll take the first leg."

***

Elyse smiled apologetically into the red lights on the TV camera. "Of course, Sir," she said politely without acknowledging the questioning Senator. "The rate of criminal infiltration into legitimate businesses since the second and third generation of mobsters like my father and his children changed their modes of operation has become so prevalent in recent years that it's sometimes difficult to tell which is which and undoubtedly accounts for a large percentage of America's 'corporate' crime. It has risen even more dramatically during this last recession because while many legitimate businesses teeter daily on the edge of bankruptcy in such a declining economy, *La Cosa Nostra* is never without funds because of the enormous income from their illegal racketeering. Of course, if their illegal activities weren't illegal, *they* would be out of business.

"In other areas, my half-sister's husband, Sal Pagano,

serves on the Board of the Sixth Federal Savings and Loan in Boston. He gained this position by helping them absorb a portfolio of bad loans they had kept rather than passing them off to Fannie Mae and Freddie Mac because they wanted to be known as a friendly, small lender, who played by the old books instead of cooking the new ones. The Boston Family also specializes in offering pre-paid cell phone distribution and one-payment credit card settlements, but the phones never get delivered and the credit card debts go unsettled.

"Frankie Garono, *Capo* of the second leading Family after my father's in New York, has controlling interest in several new oil and natural gasoline distributing companies.

"My father, through a front, which is the way these things are usually done, owns one of the most famous skyscrapers in Manhattan, a holding he was able to obtain when the former Japanese owners defaulted on their loans.

"During the heydays of Wall Street and bank bailouts several years ago, the New York and New Jersey Families established fake brokerage houses and marketed worthless stocks to unsuspecting investors, bribed other brokers, and threatened security personnel if they didn't give up lists of customers. I mean these schemes give a whole new meaning to 'vulture' and 'crony capitalism'.

"Mobsters own billions in real estate across the nation and have long been co-owners of bars, restaurants, trucking and construction firms, food and garment manufacturing companies, all legal businesses they never could have penetrated so easily without the billions of dollars pulled each year from their *illegal* racketeering. Like any money collecting institution, like any bank, they must re-invest their money, too. You've all heard of 'laundered money' I'm sure, dirty or illegal money passing through legitimate or legal hands to come out 'clean'. Well, increasingly, the country itself is becoming the Mob's laundromat'."

***

Doria remained on her knees even though they hurt terribly because the stone floor of the church was hard and cold. This time she couldn't even confess to her priest and have him intervene with the Lord for her. This time she had to deal with God alone. But she couldn't find any words. They were there: "Forgive me, Lord, my God, for I know it is a sin to take a life, but please God, understand, it is the only way . . . and I have to get to her first—"She couldn't utter the actual words. She only felt an enormous pressure inside her head, a throbbing inside her temples. The throbbing beat out the words for her: "Forgive me. Forgive me."

***

Had he understood her correctly when she said if their illegal activities weren't illegal, *the Mob* would be out of business? The Senator from Michigan wanted desperately to ask this earnest young woman if she was insinuating that the Mob's illegal activities, where they originally obtain money to fund legitimate businesses, should be made legal, but he just didn't dare. Prostitution? Unregulated gambling? Drugs? These were blasphemous in any voter's vocabulary. "Ms. Gadonni," he asked instead, "Could you give us some more specifics as to the *people* your father met with when you were still living in his home, people from this pseudo-legitimate world you speak of?"

Elyse answered cooperatively, as she had done the entire three days of her appearances, feeling not at all tired, feeling cleansed in some invigorating sort of way even though she, personally had never been a part of the filth. It was as if she had become the voice of her *true* heritage, speaking for every good and decent person of Italian lineage, who was as horrified and offended by *La Cosa Nostra* as she was. And those who weren't horrified and offended deserved to be included in her indictment, as did all non-Italians, including at least a few of the Senators in front of her now, who probably mixed with the Mob now and then on one level or another.

"Sir," she said with a touch of pseudo-genuine chagrin in her voice, "that list is extremely long. So in order to avoid monotony and time, I have compiled a *written* list that I would now like to submit to this panel. I would like to add, however—" The Senator from Nevada leaned forward in his chair. Did he detect a note of warning in her voice?— "that I have provided a copy of this list to a certain investigative reporter to assure that none of the names inadvertently become, uh, *misplaced*." Elyse smiled. The list was from Nico. She was damning her father and disseminating her friend's work at the same time. Perfect!

***

Lorgan poured more gin into the ice-filled shaker without taking his eyes off the TV monitor. He rarely drank hard liquor, but there was good reason to feel the need for more than one big martini today. Could he really trust Doria? She had lived her whole adult life in obedience to Zio. Would she be able to go through with it? A mother's love for her child was a unique phenomenon in the world of relationships. It was enduring. It was strong. Was it enough?

Lorgan drank deeply from his glass, his attention still riveted on the screen, on his loved one, praying that Doria's mother love would be strong enough.

***

The Majority Leader of the Senate rose and spoke into the red lights of the TV camera. "Thank you, Ms. Gadonni. We admit this list for our further investigation, and we thank you for your courage and patriotism in offering your extensive knowledge into our hands. We thank you, and the country thanks you. We shall adjourn for the day. 10:00 tomorrow morning, everyone, please."

As Nico guided her from the government building, one FBI agent on her other arm and another close behind, they were besieged by reporters with cameras and microphones, as they had been each day since her appearances began. Elyse's face had appeared on the Evening News and in the morning papers every day for three days running. She refused to give interviews or speak a word to anyone. The flesh-eating media would flock to her just as excitedly were she a mass murderer or a successful swindler. She wanted none of it.

She was to go back to the Hearings tomorrow for one last appearance, one she hadn't counted on, to officially present to the Senate an incredible, irrefutable documentation of her father's "acquaintances," a pictorial roll call of the most powerful Mob leaders in the country, plus the additional bonus of many "outsiders" in full color and stereophonic sound. She suffered shock when Nico informed her moments ago about her mother's offering the government both the photo album and the video of her wedding day. Evidently, her mother stated unequivocally to Nico's

Washington contact that she would give the items only into the hands of her daughter. So the FBI ensconced Doria in the same "safe house" to which she was headed now in an ordinary, brown Chevrolet, out of D.C. and into the State of Maryland.

Elyse felt fear for the first time. Her mother should not do this thing. Why? God only knows what her father would do if he finds out his wife took the album and the video. Zio must already wonder where Doria is. The farthest her mother had ever gone from home alone was to the supermarket or a nearby shopping mall for a few hours, and now she had been absent for nearly a whole day. Zio must be going crazy! Elyse turned to Nico in the car. "How did she know about your contact here in Washington? She never knew your name or anything specific about you, only that there was a college friend who had informed me of my family's criminal activities. I don't understand."

"Your mother will tell you everything you need to know," Nico answered tightly, hoping to avoid a conversation in front of the Feds and any detection of his own worries. He couldn't tell her, now, that the only way he and Lorgan could think of for the FBI to agree to install the wife of Rinaldo Gadonni in the same safe house apartment with their star witness was to provide proof of her allegiance by the offer of the wedding pictures. He couldn't tell her, now, *why* they needed to devise a way for Doria to be alone with her. And he also couldn't tell her that the blue car following them for the first thirty miles was connected to the black sedan that followed them for the second twenty miles and was connected to the green SUV following them now, or that it was the driver of this last car they were trying to save her from. Nico looked cautiously out the side view mirror. Just as Lorgan had warned in his e-mail, he recognized Dumdum when she first began to tail them. *Dumdum.* How perfectly natural, given Zio's temperament, to send one daughter to snuff out the life of the other.

The Fed sitting on the other side of Elyse nodded his head to Nico. He hadn't noticed the first two tails, but the green SUV caught his eye. "I'm watching it," he muttered.

TWENTY

SHE COULDN'T BE sure whether her mother was laughing or crying as they held each other. She only knew that Doria Gadonni was shaking uncontrollably. Elyse patted her mother's hair soothingly, sensing somehow that simple comfort was what she needed, that the shaking came from both the laughter of relief and the tears of fear.

"Mama," she asked finally. "Would you like some red wine? I have a bottle in the bedroom."

Doria dried her eyes with a trembling hand and smiled gratefully. "Thank you, Little one," she choked.

"Little one?" Elyse went to get the wine and, grabbing glasses from the kitchen, hurried back to the apartment's living room. "You haven't called me that in years."

"Haven't I?" Doria let the wine calm her. "That's funny, I always think of you that way."

Elyse felt stinging in her own eyes. "Mama, why have you come here? What are you doing giving the government your wedding pictures? Whose idea was all this?"

"It was both me and Lorgan together." Doria sipped

anxiously at her wine between words and began to pick at the food delivered on trays by their FBI guard. "You're not safe here, Little one, because of your father. Lorgan loves you, so he's devised a way for you to escape. I've come to help." She delved into her bag and placed the pills on the coffee table.

"Oh, my Little one!" Doria began to cry again. "You do forgive me, don't you? For marrying your father?" She hesitated. "For loving him, for ever having born you at all? I know you won't believe me, but I swear to you I really never knew. It's my own fault, I know, but I never, ever did. I know God won't forgive me now for what I am doing, but I need so badly to be forgiven."

Elyse gathered her mother into her arms again, crying with her this time, their mingling tears washing away their mutual pain, their unearned guilt, their unasked for tasks. "Oh, but you're so very wrong, Mama," she whispered, feeling suddenly both comforting and comforted, both little girl and grown woman. "I do believe you. I do forgive you."

"These are sleeping pills. I'll leave the bottle on our night table in the bedroom," her mother offered. "Lorgan says three should be enough because they're very strong. I'll flush the rest down the toilet in the morning, so it will look like you took the whole bottle that the FBI agent saw this morning when he checked me in here. Lorgan told me to tell you he e-mailed Nico about the plan in case you decide to follow his instructions, so he would know what to do to help us. I don't understand e-mails, but Lorgan said Nico has a Smarty phone like he does, so they can keep in constant touch with each other. Something about blueberries, I think. I guess that must be a code word or something. Anyway, it's up to you about the pills. If you take them, Nico will know what to do."

Elyse shook her head and smiled indulgently at her mother's ignorance. "You'd better rest now, Mama." Obviously Lorgan and Nico were communicating on their Blackberry cell phones, and that was positive news. She followed her mother into the bedroom, waited while she undressed and put on her nightgown in the bathroom, tucked her into one of the twin beds, and then sat on the edge of her own bed staring at the bottle as if it contained poison. What if it did? She looked over at her dear, sweet mother. Unused to so much wine, she fell asleep immediately after dinner. Doria's long, reddish hair, pulled into a bun during the day, spilled loosely onto the pillow. Asleep like this, she looked very young. Young. Pure. Innocent.

Her mother had come here to help *someone*. Of that she had no doubt. Doria Gadonni would never have set upon a mission so far from home without being instructed on how to do so by someone. It was the identity of the "someone" that bothered Elyse. Was it really her mother's idea to offer the wedding stuff in the hope that it could help in some way—*any* way—and then Lorgan's idea to use it to get her into Elyse's safe house and bring the pills? Since arriving in Washington, there had been no opportunity for Elyse to speak privately with Nico because of the always-present FBI men, so there was no way to confirm anything with him now either. Would her mother deliver anything harmful to her only child even if her husband ordered her to do it? It couldn't be! Doria was used to obeying, but not this! She would not obey her husband over God.

Then the pills must have come from Lorgan, who loved her. They must be sleeping pills, and the plan for escape her mother mentioned must be a true plan. Her mother even promised she would escape with her. They would be taken to California and then Lorgan would take them both out of the country.

But what if her father had engineered the whole thing because she was so well guarded he couldn't get to her any other way soon enough to shut her up before she gave more incriminating evidence against him? Giving the wedding stuff was of some use to the Feds but not much after she already gave Nico's long list of her father's associates to the Senate. Still, what if Zio conceived a devious plan that would *fool* both Lorgan and Doria into carrying it out? If only she could talk to Nico. This was all such a tangled web of "What ifs." Like what if her father was using both Lorgan and Doria as unsuspecting players in a scenario that would find her dead as the final curtain descended?

Her father was ruthless. She fully believed he would want her dead. But why would Zio go to all the trouble to connive a plan using both the man who loved her and the woman who bore her to kill her? Punishment to them? Revenge? No, it wasn't plausible. Zio Gadonni was a seasoned, professional killer. If he wanted her dead, he would go about it in his usual, most efficient manner, with a "hit" man pulling the trigger. He would never bother with theatrics.

Then they *were* sleeping pills. Lorgan considered three of them enough to put her under without putting her "out." Elyse shook her head at her suspicions and poured the remaining wine into her glass. It must be the strain of this whole ordeal to imagine such things. How could she ever consider that the man she loved and her own mother—no matter how weak they both may have been in the past—would conspire in any plan to hurt her? She swallowed the pills without further thought and lay back to wait for them to work.

The sinking feeling came first, and then the haziness. Then the warmth. Lorgan filled her thoughts: his light-filled, deep blue eyes, his hands gripping her waist, his mouth tasting of oranges. Part of a prayer from her childhood came into cloudy focus from seemingly nowhere in her mind. She offered it to Lorgan, no sound coming from her moving lips as she slipped into the deepest of sleeps.

"Into thy hands, I commend my soul."

TWENTY-ONE

THE FBI GUARD scanned the parking lot from a window at the end of the hallway, then reached for binoculars. Was that the same green SUV he thought might be following them yesterday afternoon on their way back from Washington? Couldn't be. It turned off the highway at least thirty miles from the safe house. Still, it sure looked the same. That's the problem, all cars look alike today. Too much of a coincidence not to be a coincidence. If anyone was following them, the last thing they'd do would be to park in the same apartment building's parking lot. Forget it.

He checked his watch: 7:30. His partner would swing by to pick them up for the morning return trip to Washington in half an hour. He unbuttoned his suit jacket, providing quick access to his shoulder holster and walked back to stand in front of the witness's door. He could hear her reporter pal moving about in his own room across the hall but detected no sounds coming from the girl's apartment. Could she and her mother have overslept?

Nico, in fact, had been up for over an hour texting back and forth to Lorgan's cousin, Nat, that Lorgan's plan was at full throttle and they needed to pin down details. With the FBI guard around to witness the intricate drama, there could be no slip-ups. The whole scene had to look natural, and everybody needed to play their part believably. The ambulance had already been "borrowed" from the hospital parking lot by Nat and his brother, Jason, and they were waiting a few blocks away until they received Nico's message to come for Elyse. Dressed in dark pants and white shirts with blue vests, they would pass as medics well enough. The get-away car to take Elyse from the ambulance was stationed a couple of miles away in a strip shopping center, where stores wouldn't open for another two hours. All he needed to do was wait for Doria's signal. Lorgan had warned Nico to watch out for her because she was timid and shy, and her present role wasn't remotely natural for her, so she might accidently foil the plan— He checked his Blackberry. The "GO" message to Nat was already typed in. All he had to do was push "Send," and Nat and his brother would move into action. He hooked the cell phone to the front of his belt, sat on the bed and stared at the door.

A woman's scream propelled the FBI guard toward his witness's door, gun drawn, just in time to keep him from falling through it as Doria flung it open, her eyes wide with fright. "I can't wake her," she sobbed. "She's dead! She's taken a whole bottle of pills."

Right on schedule. Nico came running out of his room and followed Elyse's mother and the guard back into the apartment, where they found Elyse lying still in bed, looking peacefully asleep. Doria grabbed his arm. "For God's sake, call an ambulance. Do something! Call 911!"

Nico ran to the telephone and dialed the three-digit

number. Then, turning his back to the guard, he broke the connection by pressing down on the button and shouted urgently into the receiver. "Operator, this is an emergency, we need an ambulance fast, we're at—"he turned to the guard, who was taking Elyse's pulse—"Where are we? The corner of Pastel and, what is it, Rogers?"

"Roberts," the FBI guy answered without looking up.

"Corner of Pastel and Roberts Street, operator, number 423, 6th floor. Where is the nearest hospital? Okay, King's County Hospital. How long will it take them to get here?"

Nico turned his back to the guard again, hung up the phone, and pushed "Send" on his Blackberry. Then he returned to Elyse's bedside. "Help should be here in five minutes," he whispered. "Oh, God. Is she dead?"

The FBI man rose and looked suspiciously at Doria. "Not yet. She's got a pulse, but it's pretty faint. Where did she get the pills Mrs. Gadonni? She didn't have them before, when we routinely searched her handbag."

Doria was sobbing constantly now. "They're mine," she wailed. "I always take one before bed. Elena saw me take it. I put the bottle back in my pocketbook. The security man who brought me here this morning saw it, and he could read the label and see they were a prescription made out to me. Why would she go and take them all? Why? Why?" Thank God her purse and suitcase were *all* he searched, she thought dazedly. After retrieving her luggage at the D.C. airport and before meeting Nico's contact man, she had gone to the Ladies' Room and taped the "other" thing tight to her stomach under several layers of clothing the way she'd seen in cowboy movies. But Elena's safe-house guard only looked through her bags and didn't pat her down, so the precaution was unnecessary and her ultimate mission secure.

The guard shook his head. "Maybe she didn't take them on purpose." Then as if belatedly registering the fact, "Why do you have your coat on, Mrs. Gadonni?"

Doria stopped crying and stared up at him aghast. "I am wearing my coat because I don't have a robe here." Then she continued accusingly. "Are you accusing me of trying to kill my own daughter? How could I force her to take pills? You have to swallow them yourself, and why would I run out to tell you about her and tell this young man to call an ambulance to try to save her if I wanted her dead?" She sobbed again and kept dabbing her eyes with a tissue in her right hand. No matter what, she had to have that hand free. Nico patted Doria's shoulder as if to comfort her. She was doing great.

"Maybe you tricked your daughter, and when you found she wasn't dead by morning, you decided to play it this way to throw us off your scent—"

The sounds of a siren cut him off. He grabbed Nico's arm and handed him a key. "Get downstairs and be sure no one, *no one*, gets into the elevator with you and the ambulance attendants. If there are more than two, let only two of them in. That's enough to carry this light woman. Use the key to bring the elevator straight to this floor without any stops and leave it in the lock when you get here to keep it here. Okay? Go!"

The guard bent over Elyse again and picked up her hand. The pulse was still beating but barely. "Your little girl had better not die, Mrs. Gadonni," he warned. He snapped a handcuff to Doria's left wrist—she was still crying into the tissue with her right hand—and the matching cuff to the metal headboard where she had slept. Doria pressed an elbow along the outside of her coat pocket as if she were cold. As long as he let her keep the coat on, she would be all right. She could do what she was determined to do calmly and quietly as long as she could get to her coat pocket. "Aren't you going to let me go with her to the hospital?" she whispered, certain now that she was handcuffed to the bed, she would not be allowed.

"Not on your life."

Nico and the "medics" rushed past them, and lifting Elyse's limp body onto a stretcher rushed back out again.

"God speed, Little one," Doria whispered, reaching her free hand out in an effort to touch her daughter for the last time.

The guard followed them and, locking the door to keep Doria in the apartment, he entered the elevator with Nico and the medics.

Nico looked at the FBI man in surprise. "You coming with us?"

"Hell, no, but I've got to reset this damned elevator after you leave, so it won't go beyond the fifth floor for residents who live here. I'll walk back up to our floor and wait for Al outside the apartment where the mother is, but you stick close to this girl. Al should be here in" —he looked at his watch—"ten minutes. I'll send him over to the hospital. King's County, you said. Right?" Nico nodded. "Here." The guard pulled a sheet up over Elyse's face. "Just in case anybody coming in might recognize her face from TV."

As the three men rolled Elyse's stretcher from the elevator into the lobby, which was filling up with onlookers, the Fed grabbed Nico's arm roughly. "And I mean you *stick* to this girl: elevators, operating rooms, everywhere." He returned to the elevator, set it to go straight to the fifth floor, took the key out of the lock to let it run naturally after he exited, and climbed up the inside staircase to the sixth-floor safehouse.

Hearing nothing from inside the apartment, he unlocked the door, opened it a crack, and peeked inside. His prisoner was kneeling beside the bed obviously praying. Without a word he locked her in again and walked hurriedly to the window at the end of the corridor. The green SUV was still there. He waited until the ambulance sped away from the curb—no one followed it—and then returned grimly to his post.

Almost immediately, he heard sounds. A woman's high heels clicking on the stairs? Jesus! What now? Doria's guard unbuttoned his jacket and waited tensely. He checked his watch. Seven minutes till Al, who had his own elevator key to the safe floor. What the fuck now—?

Claretta struggled with two bags of groceries in the stairwell. Cops were so easy to find it made you sick, damn near took the fun away. Didn't anybody else wonder why, in a six-story apartment building, the elevator wouldn't go past the fifth floor? Now she didn't have to wait until the Feds left the building with Elena. She could do the job here. Much cleaner this way, out of view from anyone else standing around. She stumbled out of the stairwell's doorway into the hall and stopped in her tracks, noticing the FBI man in surprise. No surprises, even. The jerkheads always stood blocking the door like that, with their arms crossed in front of them to hide their gun. The jerk spoke tersely to her.

"Can I help you?"

Pretending nervousness, Claretta edged back toward the escape route of stairs. "Well, I don't know. Since you're blocking the door to my apartment, maybe I should be asking you that question."

The guard frowned. The woman was very pretty, dressed nicely, her long black hair tied back with a scarf, and her brown eyes intelligent but wary of him. Both arms full of groceries. Totally unthreatening. Must be some honest mistake. "Well, Miss," he raised an eyebrow. "How can this be your door when my own sister lives in this apartment? That's who I'm waiting for. Now, let's try to figure out where you think you are."

Claretta looked at the lettering on the door behind him. "B," she said in exasperation. "B. B. 5B. Now, what's going on here? First the lobby with all those people watching them take a dead person out. I can't stand it when people flock to see accidents and things, can you? And then so many other residents pushing into the elevator—Impossible! I walked up all five floors rather than wait in line. Now you tell me I don't know where I live?"

"Wait. Wait. No more." The security man grinned in amusement. "There's your problem. You're on the *sixth* floor, not the *fifth* floor. This is 6B."

Claretta laughed. A delightful, tinkling kind of laugh. She had plenty of time. Louie and Joey would stall the second jerkhead, the driver, if he came into the building. She watched the FBI jerk laugh at her laugh. "Listen," she said, "since you're just waiting around anyway, would you be a real gent and help me back down with these groceries? I'm just beat. To think I walked an extra floor with all this stuff."

"Sorry, can't do that for you. I'd like to, but I can't take the chance of missing my sister."

Claretta moved toward him quickly. "Well, at least hold these heavy things while I get keys out of my purse." She shoved the bulging bags into his arms. "That way, when I get back down to my own door I, at least, won't have to put them down and pick them back up again." She fished in her handbag, and then laughing again with that enchanting tinkling sound, she pulled out a gun and silently shot the FBI guy in the throat.

Before he fell completely to the floor with groceries spilling all around, she found keys in his pocket, and by the time he died, she quietly unlocked the door to the apartment he was guarding and stepped inside.

Elena was kneeling by the bed, leaning into it, her long reddish-auburn hair loose down the back of her coat. Well, Claretta thought, she has a lot to pray about. She took her stance in the open doorway leading to the bedroom and without saying a word, poured the five remaining bullets left in her gun soundlessly into her half-sister's back.

The force of the shots tilted the body over against the edge of the bed, looking like some staccato scene from a silent movie. Only then, as it clinked against metal, did Claretta notice that one of Elena's hands was cuffed to the bed's headboard. Only then did she see the pillow wedged between the body and the mattress edge, a pillow that, when she shoved the body completely aside, was already covered with blood. Blood from—Claretta clenched her teeth in shock and anger—blood from *Doria*! Dead by her own hand. A pistol tumbled to the floor—

Overcome with horror and fear, Claretta slumped, breathless, against the door frame. She knew she should retrieve it and return it to her father. But did she dare? She had never touched it. *Nobody* ever touched it. Nobody except Doria, evidently. Because no one—*no one*—was allowed to touch anything on Zio's bureau.

What should she do now? She had failed her Hit mission. When ordered from the top, this could have dire consequences. She knew the penalty, and her father was of such ruthless temperament he would likely institute it— "mercy" was not in his vocabulary. But she failed only because Elena wasn't there to be whacked, so what would that mean? If she returned it, she would have to tell Zio that Doria was dead by her own hand. What kind of extra rage would that cause? And toward whom? The one who also shot five bullets into his dead wife's back?

On the run herself, now, Claretta tripped over the dead man in the hallway in her frenzy to race back down six flights of stairs and away from the scene and her father's favorite gun.

TWENTY-TWO

SHE HAD A THROBBING headache, but she didn't care. It told her she was alive. Elyse opened her eyes ever so slightly, so she could see kind of hazily without drawing attention to her wakefulness. She was in the back seat of a car and covered to her chin with a white sheet. There was no one else in the vehicle except the driver, a clean-cut, middle-aged man. Quietly, she pulled up the edge of the sheet. There was some writing on the hem: King's Memorial Hospital. Hospital? Had she been in a hospital?

Suddenly her eyes opened all the way, startled, as a white florist box landed lightly on her stomach. "Lorgan said to give this to you when you woke up, so you won't be afraid of me," the driver smiled pleasantly into the rear view mirror. "I'm his cousin Jason."

Elyse sat up feeling funny in her stomach, her headache still with her. She opened the box, then closed it again. She must be sick. The gardenia's fragrance was nauseating. Her favorite flower smelled like a funeral home.

The driver flipped another package back. "Here, eat this

yogurt. Make you feel better. Even a few sleeping pills that strong can give you a big-time hangover."

So he knew about the pills. "Where is my mother?"

"The Feds wouldn't let her go in the ambulance with you, but I left the other 'ambulance attendant' behind to go back for her. Not to worry, my brother will bring her to you safe and sound."

"And Nico?"

"He had to stay there and play the game. We left him tied up in the 'borrowed' ambulance when we ditched it. We called for another ambulance from the same hospital with a real emergency call, so it would arrive at the safe house within ten minutes of our own departure. That way, when the cops find *our* ambulance, Nico won't be a suspect in your abduction. He couldn't know he was putting you in anything but the ambulance he called for, right?"

"You say you 'ditched' it?"

"Just slang for leaving it on a lonely road, honey. Nobody will hurt Nico. Nobody will get hurt at all. Lorgan's orders. After that testimony of yours, everybody will think your *father* arranged to have you picked up one way or another. Nico says you were being followed to the safe house, and nobody else besides your mother and Nico knew about the pills, so that story will spin."

Lorgan, she thought. Oh, if only Lorgan had been telling the truth about getting away together. But who else would know about the gardenia? It had to be Lorgan. "Exactly where are we going now?" she demanded.

"We're driving to Philly in case the airports around Washington are under surveillance. Then we take a flight to San Francisco, pick up another car and drive to L.A. and Lorgan. But even with all these precautions, you've been seen on TV, so there's a short wig for you in here." He pulled a paper bag from the glove compartment and tossed it back. What name is on your I.D. for the airport?"

"Elyse Gannon. I had my name changed legally a couple of years ago."

"Good. Everyone who interrogated you or saw you on TV will only know of Elena Gadonni. You were smart to use your father's name for that. Good girl—"

Elyse put the wig on and settled back to eat her yogurt. Well, whatever happened now would happen. At least she had done it. *She* had let the government and the public know who her father was. She—*Zio's own daughter*—had revealed *specifics* regarding his activities and those of a whole lot of the next generation as well. Law enforcers knew before she appeared at the Hearings that her father was a Boss, of course, but they didn't know he was Boss of all Bosses, "first among firsts," as Nico said. The Feds were never before able to *prove* anything, even things they already suspected about Zio. Well, she had shown them the road to that proof. She told them where to look: into his *legitimate* businesses. With smart digging, they would now find enough there, surely, to ruin him. As he tried to ruin her.

The man pulled off the highway into a service area but stopped the car and turned around to face her before proceeding to the gas pumps. He pulled a handgun from inside his coat and held it up, not pointed at her but flat in his hand for her to see.

"Look, Ms. Gannon, Lorgan ordered nobody's to be hurt in this tricky caper, but please try to appreciate my position. It's my job to deliver you to California. So just trust that I come from Lorgan and Lorgan loves you and will save you from your father. Don't try to get away. Okay?"

TWENTY-THREE

LORGAN STUCK HIS HEAD in the phone booth to make his third call in three hours, sweat bulleting his forehead. He couldn't use his cell or home phone for this, so he'd driven to a movie theater ten miles from his house that still had a row of pay telephones near the restrooms. The phones weren't the old fashioned standing booths but adhered to a wall with partitioned-off sections that gave some privacy and left no trail of the caller. The overpowering odor of popcorn was making him sick to his stomach, so he drank Coke after Coke, but nothing helped. Each time he called, he waited impatiently for an answer that Elyse was alright, and even though the "booths" weren't enclosed like when he was a kid, it was as if the past merged ever more fully with the present. He felt again the nervousness of making a mistake when talking to his father in the old phone booths, blending into the fear of the priest in the confines of the confessional and ending with his frantic worry over Elyse, the last more precious to him than even God had ever been.

He fitted more coins into the slots, praying for this call to be answered, which would mean that Jason had crisscrossed his trail well enough to be safely back in California and was close by. Finally—

"Jason, here."

"Is she all right?"

"Yes, Elyse is sitting right beside me here in the car."

"Her mother?"

"Negative. The Feds wouldn't let her go in the ambulance, so Nico sent Nat to retrieve her. Gotta go, lots of traffic."

Negative? *What happened?* Negative was a code word meaning *dead,* as in "negative existence." Obviously Jason couldn't talk with Elyse in the car. Doria had been so brave. If she'd come along with Elyse as planned, he would have taken the responsibility of sneaking her safely out of the country to a distantly-related, non-Mafia Jewish family's retreat in the Caribbean, a secure place he'd ferreted out years ago and unknown even to his mother. Doria's chances of survival there would have been good, but she might have resisted going without Elyse, raising other problems in an already fragile situation. Regardless, the issue was no longer relevant. "Negative" meant she'd been hit, and "went to *retrieve* her" meant to retrieve her *body.*

"Understood," he said, dry tears stinging his eyes for the loss of such an innocent and beautiful spirit that was Doria, who had somehow lost her own life in trying to save her daughter. She, the most unlikely of individuals, had managed to outwit her husband and give the pills to Elyse, providing the method to get her out of harm's way. He would learn details later, but his whole being felt an indelible and irreversible pain at the loss of this innocent woman he had adored as a young man. "You can bring

Elyse directly here," he instructed his cousin.

At least he and the woman he loved would be together soon. The only woman he ever loved. Lorgan drove his car slowly back to his house, his mind deep in thought. Should he tell Elyse about her mother or not? Nat and Nico would arrange a proper burial, he knew. But where? Back to Italy, he decided, where Doria's purity was untainted. He'd e-mail Nico when he got home.

Zio had let Lorgan return to California three days after Elyse began her appearances. The crime boss didn't need him anymore. He knew where his daughter was. Lorgan guessed Zio made him stay for those few days to observe him while he watched Elyse on TV to see if he could glean anything suspicious from Lorgan's expressions. Lorgan managed stoicism throughout. When he arrived home and automatically checked his house, he found the dogs groggy from tranquilizing darts no doubt, and the telephones and every room in the house bugged. They clearly didn't trust him.

The dogs were fine now, and Zio would certainly know by this late hour of Elyse's disappearance and Doria's demise, so he would send someone sooner or later to check his house again, but that was all right. Later, both he and Elyse would be gone. Sooner, the dogs would let him know. There would still be time.

Jason could tell him details of Doria's death in private. Then he'd decide what to say—or not—to Elyse. By now Zio would definitely have ordered both Lorgan and Elyse whacked any time, any place, any way, with an open contract on their lives. The Old Man *had* to order the killings not only out of personal revenge but also to save his position at the top, if it wasn't already lost by Elyse's testimony and Doria's incriminating "gifts." The Feds would go after Zio directly, now, because they had enough new avenues to explore and come up with plenty of hard evidence to indict him, so it was also perfectly plausible for other wannabe "Boss of all Bosses" to try and rub Zio out because of his precarious position.

Beyond all that, Nico would soon have hoards more info to use however he wished to assure that Zio and many of his associates and underlings would soon be out of the picture one way or another. Nevertheless, the open Hit order for both his and Elyse's lives would remain *the* top priority for Zio right now no matter what he had to face later: the slammer or even death. There was no way Zio hadn't concluded that Lorgan scripted Elyse for her testimony. Who else? Zio didn't know about Nico, and she had sung like a knowledgeable canary.

Mobsters killed members of their own families when required by circumstance or deceit. But not often and never in their own homes. He well remembered the time when he was lunching with his father at a little Italian hangout in L.A., and the current California Boss came over to their table so timidly, bringing a bottle of red wine with him. "Frankie, Frankie, you have-ta help me," he whined to his first lieutenant. "Zio called me and says my kid's 'gotta go'." The guy was crying, this tough bird who made his bones in the old days, he was crying. "I can't kill my own kid, you understand? I don't know why my son done this thing, skimming off the top from Zio after plenty warnings. He don't need money. It must be 'cause he's running around with dames. He hardly comes home to his wife anymore. He's doing drugs himself, too, but I can't kill my own kid! Tonight I'm taking the Red Eye to New York and plead with Zio tomorrow morning, but you call him first, Frankie. You're an old friend of Zio's from babyhood. You call him first and soften him up for me. Okay, Frankie?"

As soon as the old guy left, Lorgan's father called Zio from a phone booth in the restaurant, and Zio let the old guy's kid live in return for his father's graceful retirement. The old guy retired, Frankie Cantrelli killed the son, and Zio very happily installed his childhood pal as Boss of the California Family. . .and unhappily put Lorgan in line.

Still troubled by so many things, Lorgan walked through his home for the last time, reaching out once in a while to caress a white marble sculpture, the frame of a painting, or a hand-etched window pane—

Even as a youngster, he heard his father and other mobsters talking about their "jobs." Sons were not kept in the dark about criminal activities. He had lived quietly in that dirty world for forty-six years. Since Elyse came into his life, the same question plagued him over and over. Even though he stayed on the outskirts of Mob activity by going into show business, why had he never *really* questioned any of the dirt? Why had he never summoned the guts to repudiate his family like Elyse did? He even had the Jewish card to play. Why hadn't he at least tried that?

In the end, *he* was guilty for Elyse's present, dangerous position. If he had refused the order to become part of the plot to trick her back into the Family, she would never have testified, and none of this would have happened. If he had left his own Family, Zio wouldn't have been able to use him against Elyse. She was the honest, brave, and innocent one whereas he and others like him never rebelled like she did. Plenty of *Cosa Nostra* children hated their fathers and stayed out of their way but never actually repudiated their families and *never* ratted. So even if they never took an active part in that crooked and blood-stained world, he and all those like him were also, in their own passive ways, responsible for the continuation of Mob activity. Why?

Because in some regard or another we benefit ourselves from that world.

At a certain point in the past, he now admitted to himself, it didn't matter how he suffered guilt or wanted out. He had condoned too much by his silence, the vow of *Omerta*. He deserved what lay ahead. But Elyse was innocent of any wrongdoing, even passive or implicit. When she learned of her father's criminality, she confronted him, judged him to be evil, and left the Family. What courage!

If *he* had not agreed to set in motion the scenario that eventually led to her testimony, she *still* would remain removed from her father's wrath.

She walked toward him, then, followed by the one man he could trust. They grew up as boys together and loved each other as brothers. He nodded a warm thanks to Jason, realizing that although his Jewish cousin's own hands were clean, he, too, bore guilt for the sin of compliance.

Lorgan waited until he heard sounds of Jason's car fade in the distance before reaching up somewhat shyly and removing Elyse's wig, releasing her burnished-red length of hair to fall like a spreading fire around her shoulders. Her eyes held questions.

"Come, we'll have a late lunch together," he offered. "You need solid food to get your stomach back to normal. I made some chicken breast and rice. Do you feel okay with that?" Elyse nodded. Lorgan took her hand and led them to an umbrella table by the swimming pool, where he had their meal already prepared and waiting. Both dogs growled an affectionate greeting to Elyse, their tails wagging happily to see her again. Lorgan noticed that her hand felt cold. . .and bare.

"Where is your engagement ring?" he asked slowly.

Elyse looked at her left hand. The diamond ring was gone. She shook her head, wondering, and then realized. "It must have come off when they were wrapping those sheets around me? Or maybe when I was wrestling to get out of the sheets in Jason's car? It must be either in the ditched ambulance or the car. Can we call Jason?"

Lorgan picked up his cell and made the call. "We'll leave this evening," he said quietly to Elyse.

"On a sailboat, perhaps? One named 'Dreamer'? *That* would be a dream come true."

Would that such a dream was possible, he thought. Aloud, he continued in a low but steady tone: "Elyse, I know the doubts that must be disturbing you, but I must take you away, far away to a place where Zio can never touch us. He has no choice, now, but to chase us anywhere and everywhere until we're gone for good. You must know this."

Elyse nodded in agreement. How strong Lorgan was. Now she must be strong, too.

Jason came on the line. "Did you find Elyse's ring in the car?"

Jason ignored the question and got to the point, reporting Doria's suicide. When his brother, Nat, went to get her, she was already dead from shooting herself in the gut with a pistol. There were also five hollow-point bullets in her back, and the Fed guarding her was dead in the hallway with the same kind of bullet that was in the mother's back. Nico took all the wedding stuff. Didn't want the Feds to have it until he could think it through. Thought he might be able to do more damage with the evidence himself. That okay with you? If not, e-mail him what else to do. I have her diamond. Will bring it over tomorrow."

Lorgan steeled his voice while his heart sank. "Understood. Then everything's okay. Thanks. Take care of the dogs." He set the phone back on the table, his mind reeling, and then decided not to tell Elyse anything he heard. Given his plan, what would be served by hurting her with such horrific news?

Forcing himself to smile and speak calmly, Lorgan reported the lie. "Jason's brother and Nico got your mother. They're already on a boat to the Caribbean where one of my non-Mafia Jewish family has a place no one knows about and where Doria can live in peace. My *good* family will take care of her, so don't worry. But to find *us,* especially since Claretta failed to kill you, Zio will send out an endless search into every corner of the world, so you must go with me wherever I say, even if you don't want to, even if you don't love me anymore. Because I still love you more than life itself, and it's my fault you came into such danger by following your father's orders to manage you. It's because of that and many other errors in my life that it is I alone who must save you from him. *Because it's my fault.* Because I love you so and. . . I could never stand to see you tortured when they eventually find us, and ghastly drawn-out torture before death *is* what he will order. I would gladly trade my life for yours, but he wants both of us now. Jason has your ring."

"But if it's safe in the Caribbean, why can't we join my mother and the 'other' part of your family?"

"Zio won't try to find your mother. Once he finds out about the wedding stuff she gave to the Feds, he can save face by saying she was trying to protect her only child and fled afterward. Even a butcher such as he can understand that and explain it to his 'friends', especially because your mother was so docile and delicate. But he will never let *us* go, because you have put him in the highly vulnerable position to be jailed for the rest of his life or wiped out by his own kind. He will blame me for that, too, because he will assume I told you what to say and was in on your decision to talk. I'm sure the open contract on both of us is already issued. The whole of the *Cosa Nostra* network will leave no stone unturned to find us.

He stopped talking abruptly. She was smiling. Incredibly, she was smiling, soft tears clouding her dark brown eyes, but the glow of her smile shining through the clouds. She raised her champagne glass and held it steadily in the air, toasting him. "I love you, Lorgan, and I will come with you, wherever you say. Gladly I will follow you. I forgive you. I told you that once before. Now you have to forgive yourself. You did what you had to do, and the reason I forgive you is because if you hadn't followed my father's orders, we would never have met and fallen in love, and loving you is worth more to me than anything else in my life, even more than my career that we almost created.

"And remember, I testified willingly, knowing the risk to both of us. So I did what *I* had to do. I will never regret my decision whatever the consequences because I have set in motion the destruction of at least the head of an evil octopus whose tentacles are strangling so many innocent people in this blessed country. It may take years for the Feds to finally snare him based on the evidence my mother and I offered, but whatever his future, my father will live with the knowledge that his own flesh and blood condemned *and* destroyed him. I shall always be proud to have rendered justice to that evil man. On top of that, if as you say *Claretta* was given a direct Hit order and failed to succeed as she obviously did, then the merciless bastard will not think twice before killing his one other daughter in order to save face within the syndicate. As a further dramatic show of his ballsy killer power, he will probably send Reno to do the deed just to make sure everyone understands he is still Boss. Then as my final reward, an evil father will have ordered the Hit on an evil daughter, and an evil brother will kill his own sister. So if my mother—his prized wife—has left him, which alone will drive him crazy, and the rest of that vile Gadonni house of cards falls, whatever *our* future, I am more than satisfied with both of us."

He rose quickly but walked slowly over to her, returning her serene smile with a depth of gratitude for her forgiveness that she hoped she would never see again. Taking her hand—warm now—he led her into the house and up the Lucite stairs into his bedroom. Undressing her slowly, garment after garment, one at a time, he kissed each newly exposed portion of her body separately, pressing his lips for long moments into each treasured spot as if he were taking a permanent imprint of its touch, its smell—a memory of every part of her totality until memory was no more.

She felt her body answer his. Totally.

It was dusk when they walked together—she in a long, white satin nightgown and her favorite gold-mesh slippers, and he barefoot in a white silk robe—back to the patio to finish their champagne. He walked over to the parapet on the ocean side and leaned over to gather a handful of fresh gardenias.

Only when she followed him and looked up into his eyes as he offered her the flowers did she see them—

Tears glistening in his deep blue eyes.

Her breath caught suddenly in her throat. "Take care of the dogs," he said to Jason. A moment of defiant rebellion— her passionate love of life, of the music of living, of her love for him— flashed from her own eyes. Then, understanding shaped her mouth into a firm, accepting smile.

"Lorgan," she said, forcing brightness into her voice, "Let's get married now. Here. Just the two of us," she hesitated, "unless you think your God wouldn't like it."

"There is no God," Lorgan stated flatly. "Because if there were, he would not allow *you* ever to suffer."

She took the flowers from him and held them solemnly in front of her like a bridal bouquet "I, Elyse Gannon, take you Lorgan Cantrell," she smiled at the names—their chosen names—and he smiled back, as the last rays of the sun danced in her eyes, "as my lawful, wedded husband, to love and to cherish because I love you," she hesitated briefly, "until death do us part."

"And I, Lorgan Cantrell take you, Elyse Gannon, to be my wife, now and forever, here. . . and in heaven. . .because I love you and only you."

Their kiss tasted of champagne, it smelled of gardenias. Sealing the past, it dissolved the past, and saluting the future, it created the future even if there was none—

Elyse walked to the cabana, inserted a nickel into the jukebox, and made one selection, understanding at long last why this particular song was included. It was an articulation of his most private yearnings, yearnings he had never acted upon until now, loving her— Then she returned to her husband and danced with him, singing softly into his ear:

"To dream ... the impossible dream ...To fight ... the unbeatable foe ...To bear ... with unbearable sorrow ...To run ... where the brave dare not go ...To right ... the unrightable wrong ...To love ... pure and chaste from afar ...To try ... when your arms are too weary ...To reach ... the unreachable star

*This is my quest, to follow that star ... No matter how hopeless,
no matter how far ... To fight for the right, without question or
pause ... To be willing to march into Hell, for a Heavenly
cause...*

*And I know if I'll only be true, to this glorious quest,
That my heart will lie peaceful and calm, when I'm laid to my
rest ...
And the world will be better for this: That one man, scorned and
covered with scars, Still strove, with his last ounce of courage,
To reach ... the unreachable star ..."*

When the song was finished, she picked up her
gardenias and stepped cautiously but deliberately up onto
the narrow ledge surrounding the patio. "Now! That may
be your theme song, but this is mine!" And she sang,
smiling defiantly and holding the gardenias as if they were
a microphone.

*"The world's a sweet balloon, toss it in the air, turn it in your
hand. The world is round and wonderful— Sun and stars and
singing, castles in the sand. Valentines and fireflies, their
wonder is splendiferal if you open up your eyes —
It's all yours, night and day. So review it, remake it, but live it
don't fake it.
Time's a friendly tune, play it with a flare. Ups and downs and
all-arounds, the music's light and fanciful —
Mornings are beginnings, afternoons a joy. Evenings can be
loving things, awhirl or lackadaisical, a day can be a toy.
It's all yours, night and noon, So-o spin it or bounce it but never
renounce it-
Sweet, Sweet World, Sweetmeat world. It can be a balloon —
This old wor —"*

Suddenly she looked down over the edge of the parapet and wavered, the flowers falling all around her—

"Lorgan!" she screamed, her eyes wild with fear.

He rushed over to her, and as he had on that day long ago, lifted her down to safety and held her enclosed in his arms for many silent minutes.

When she stopped shaking and he was certain she was calm, he guided her back up onto the parapet, where they stood together, looking only into each other. Elyse broke the silence. "Which way do we go tonight?" she asked, sweeping one arm confidently out over the ocean a hundred feet below. "Into the sun or away from it?"

"Toward the sun. Always toward the sun, my darling, my beloved wife."

She took his hand and held onto it very tightly. "Did we ever have a chance, Lorgan? I would never have returned to the Family even if we got married because of real love. So could we ever have stopped my father from ruining our lives? Even before? Even if I hadn't testified and brought both of us to this. . .ultimate moment?"

He whirled to her, searching her eyes. *She knew.* "No," he responded softly.

She smiled gently, forgivingly into his face.

"I love you, Lorgan."

"I love you Elyse, my love, my wife."

He gathered her closely and firmly into his arms then, feeling her hair brush against his face, smelling her skin and the fragrance of her favorite flowers hovering in the air. He kissed her tenderly, lengthily, lovingly, taking her very breath into his care before, still holding her locked into his embrace, still protecting her life with his own until life was no more for both of them, he stepped decisively off the ledge.

***

The tide was at its height. The sun set slowly as if sinking reluctantly into the sea, refusing again and again to give up its light to the darkness. But at last, slipping below the horizon with a grace equal to its struggle, it gave way and released the earth to the cool, healing touch of the moon. It was a full moon, rising effortlessly to its summit, spreading its silver rays over the water and guarding the night with its light until the next sunrise.

EPILOGUE

NICO WALKED PAST several workmen into the interior of the club. He didn't know quite why he felt the need to come here, to fly all the way from New York to stand where she sang. He didn't know why and he didn't care why.

They were tearing it down. Elyse had told the Senate committee about Paulie's drug bar. He watched as they removed plush booths and shiny tables and ripped velvet from the walls. He heard the location was taken over by a fast food company. He was glad. Bright colors and busy lines would mercifully wipe out any memory of what might have been.

Maybe he had come here hoping that being in the presence of Elyse's past he could decide what to do now. The recording Elyse made on the plane to Washington containing certain information not mentioned during the Hearings was locked safely in the file cabinet of his New York office. Alongside it was a key to a post office box in LA., sent to him by Lorgan along with a short note saying he left Nico pages and pages of inside information about

Mob activities that might help Nico in some of his future investigations. What should he do with these things? He could give them to the FBI along with Doria's wedding video and photo album or he could release them directly to the public. But if he published on his own little Blogsphere, he might just as well have jumped off the cliff with Elyse and Lorgan in their double suicide.

According to the media, Lorgan's cousin Jason was the one who reported them missing. He was also the last to see them alive when he dropped Elyse off at Lorgan's home late in the afternoon of their disappearance. He said he subsequently returned the next morning with a diamond ring he found in his car, but neither of them was there. Lorgan's sports car was still in the garage. The house was unlocked and undisturbed, but stale leftovers of a meal were found on a poolside table. There was a large scattering of wilted gardenias on the white marble parapet that edged the patio's ocean-side perimeter, so Elyse or Lorgan, or both of them, must have been on that parapet to obtain the flowers, and that low ledge dropped off straight down into the ocean a hundred feet below.

The police found no bodies, but the tide had been at its height the evening before, and anything near shore would have been swept out to sea when it subsided by morning. They found only one gold-mesh, high-heeled, woman's slipper wedged between two large rocks below. They couldn't prove a suicide without bodies, but that conclusion about Elyse's disappearance seemed obvious to the police because of her Senate testimony against her Mobster father. Nothing of Lorgan could be found at all, but Nico knew in his heart that Lorgan loved her too much to let her die alone. He fingered Elyse's diamond ring that Jason sent to him as a remembrance and he now wore around his neck

174

on a chain inside his shirt. When he returned to New York, he would lock it in the file cabinet along with everything else, but he wanted this possession of hers close to him on this pilgrimage.

At first Nico had felt anger toward Elyse for taking the most cowardly way out, especially after her courageous stand before the Senate. He was also angry at her for leaving him alone to fight their battle. But then he realized through the same thought process Lorgan must have followed that there was no other choice for them. No matter where they went in the world, Zio would never cease hunting them down. Even if the Feds arrested him based on Elyse's testimony, Zio would make sure an open contract would be sent out even if he was behind bars himself. And then their deaths would have been ugly. This way, they at least did it their own way: quickly and together.

Unfortunately, they left him such a formidable legacy that his own safety in any deepening investigative reporting lay only with a large newspaper, one protected by prominence the same way a deserted street is protected by lights. Probably one associated with a cable TV news network for wider coverage. But most of the big media players were themselves beset with politics, cover-ups, and power plays. He found that out when he worked for one before. Found that even the clean could become dirty and the accusers could be guilty.

He wandered over to the modernistic jukebox and inserted two quarters which paid for one song. Would new owners leave it here for kids to listen to while they munched on burgers and fries? Most of the music selections were typical blasts of hard Rock-Soul stuff, but there was one song of Elyse's own composition from her one and only CD album: "The World's a Sweet Balloon." He pressed the button, and her luscious voice filled the broken-down room. Then he knew why he had come: to be where she had been happiest, to hear her sing. . . here. He would never forget her. Would her father and *La Cosa Nostra*? Would the Senators or the headline-seeking media broadcasters who tried to sensationalize her? Her voice was full of radiant energy. "The World's A Sweet Balloon. Toss it in the air. Turn it in your hand. The world is round and wonderful—" Nico smiled in spite of his grief. Yes. That's how Elyse saw the world. *Sweet.*

"No," he vowed quietly to the voice coming from the jukebox. "No one will forget you because I will never let them." The Internet would be best for spreading his articles, but too much on the Net wasn't true. Skeptical people wouldn't take his stories seriously or turn them into melodramas. But he could physically verify the contents of his pieces by letting an *Editor* hear and see with his own ears and eyes Elyse's additional, recorded testimony, Lorgan's notes, and the wedding stuff. Then a big media outfit would glory in taking credit for all the Scoops.

The Mob wouldn't wipe *him* out because his name would become famous fast, so although he would surely get death threats, his actual death would only cause more investigations and arrests. They would "go to the mats" and stay hidden from the Feds for awhile. Then they would *have* to give up some top and middle-level men and re-organize again, all of which would strike more serious blows and further weaken their power. So, okay, he *would* go back to the big info outlets and put up with what's wrong with them in order to gain what's right: a voice. A *loud* voice to question, to inform, to expose, to indict not only legally but *morally*. Grabbing a plank of wood from the floor, he laid it on top of the machine and feverishly began to make notes.

Who really *was* guilty for Elyse's death? Lorgan? Elyse, herself, by giving in to suicide? The Mob? Or was the whole damned country to blame on some level for the creation and continuation of a criminal culture where innocents like Elyse are the ultimate victims?

Start with *La Cosa Nostra*, itself, a national crime "institution" that came about in an organized fashion out of otherwise loose, ethnic gangs because of the *government's* making liquor sales against the law in 1919 by passing the Eighteenth Amendment to the Constitution. The National Prohibition Act: the first and only Act ever to be repealed as it was in 1933 but also *the* Act that set precedent for the plethora of federal laws since then that the government created to outlaw various products or activities, which resulted not only in driving the products or activities underground but also by providing a black-market soil where criminals would always flourish. The Mob by illegal force and the government by legal force both interfering with choices that should be left to individuals in a free country, both *directly* guilty.

Next, any knowing family member of a mobster, who associates in any way voluntarily with their criminal relatives. Indirect, but guilty, too, because personal morality *must* trump blood relations.

Third and still within the center of the circle, people willing to actually become social *friends* of Mob members. Guilty by association.

Fourth and maneuvering around the fringe of the circle, the sort of second-tier criminal, who although not a Mob member himself commonly hangs around the edges and picks up the scraps of residual crime propagated first by the Mob. Guilty.

Next, or maybe *first*, politicians who support legislation making activities practiced by mankind since history began *illegal*—prostitution, gambling, drugs—activities not one of which, no matter how low some of them might be, when entered into voluntarily by adult men and woman infringe upon the individual rights of another single human being— Yes, by God: Guilty.

Next—who's counting anymore?—legitimate businessmen who deal in any way with mobsters knowingly and voluntarily. Guilty.

Politicians—again!—and judges and D.A.s and cops and *defense* attorneys, who take money or favors and help a killer go free. Doubly guilty.

The ripples widen: *Any* person, the hangers-on, no matter how respectable or honest their own behavior, who orbit socially around criminals of any sort, looking the other way from the truth or getting some peculiar thrill or neurotic sense of power from their shady connections. Sick and guilty.

Artists, writers, movie-makers, TV show producers and directors, advertisers, actors, publishers, newspapers, distributors, *anyone* who *glamorizes* or *sensationalizes* the underworld in any way. *Romanticizing* evil *is* evil. Inexcusable and guilty.

Every person who deals with criminals knowingly and voluntarily on any level that would legitimatize them. Guilty.

And any person who, even though not through supportive action on his own part, *fails to judge* if only in his own mind and fails to name evil when faced with it directly or indirectly or vicariously— This, perhaps, was the most subtle and venal in its own way, *the failure to judge*. Oh, you individuals one and all: Guilty.

All guilty. Right down the list and right back up it again, all paying for their actions or their support or even their evasions in varying degrees, not always paying according to Man's laws but inescapably paying according to the Laws of Reality in mentally eroding ways: moral, self esteem, and psychological deterioration.

But, Nico slipped a dollar into the machine and pushed the same button twice—he needed to hear her singing, *alive*—there are *innocent* people, and they pay, too, and their sentences are *not* earned but the result of birth or accident, or getting in the way, or acting unknowingly. They pay for the crimes large and small of all the others on the list because they pay with higher prices for commodities, with fear on unsafe streets, with lost businesses, with threatened families, with crippled limbs, with— A rain of tears began to pour unchecked down Nico's cheeks. The board fell to the floor. With. . .their. . .lives!

Who were the innocent? They should be speaking up, condemning the guilty not winking at them. Were there any at all? How many? Who? Elyse! Elyse!

The workmen halted their activities abruptly at the sound, turning to stare at the young stranger who had earlier been wandering around and to see his fist smashed through the glass window of the jukebox, stilling the music, his face drenched with tears from the pain.

It was at that exact moment when a young black man entered the room. Running to Nico, Milo Simms dislodged Nico's arm and dragged him to the Men's Room to run water over his wounds and bind up his arm with his own ripped-off tee shirt before rushing him to the hospital.

***

The two young men stood together on the patio of Lorgan's home. Milo had gone to the Chicago club for the same reason Nico had, to be again where Elyse was happiest. He'd brought his trumpet to play along with her song on the jukebox there, the place where he was her musical backup in life. Playing along with the album at home after he heard the news wasn't enough. The two had become friends during Nico's recovery, reliving and sharing memories about good times gone.

A month after Elyse's and Lorgan's disappearance, Nico heard through his sources that Lorgan's home was up for sale. When he told Milo, the horn player wanted to go to California and have a last look at the house where he and his whole group had learned so much. Milo said he would never forget Lorgan's relentless pushing and coaxing, demanding the best from each of them to lead them to the top of their playing and performing. And it was there, during that grueling month that Lorgan had begun to transform the lovely young Elyse into the fullness of womanhood by his coaching and, later, by his love.

Nico had never been to Malibu, but when they arrived Milo said that everything about Lorgan's place looked the same: White and bright and beautiful. The house was locked, but they walked around the exterior and looked through the many floor-to-ceiling windows, while Milo explained this and that. They went out to the swimming pool, where Milo said Lorgan swam his miles and made Elyse swim every day as well—they were both strong swimmers—and they looked around there and through the window into the cabana with the antique jukebox where Elyse took her dance lessons every morning. At last the pair walked over to the parapet and carefully stepped up onto it to look out over the sea that had swallowed their friends.

Milo raised his horn to his lips to play a farewell. . . and stopped —

Nico turned to him, bewildered. "What's the matter? What were you going to play?"

Milo grabbed the Sotheby real estate brochure full of color photos and specifics regarding the property from Nico's hand. The house was up for sale with or without its contents, the contents not purchased by the buyer of the home to be auctioned off. The flyer listed the most important of Lorgan's assets, featuring the most expensive: the large painting and sculpture collection, the custom-designed, one-of-a-kind piano, his exotic Aston Martin, his twin-engine plane. . . Milo went over the list again. "What about the sailboat?" he wondered aloud.

"What boat? Nothing was ever said by anyone about a boat. The cops didn't find a boat when they came here to investigate."

Milo pointed to the ocean. "It was always moored maybe a couple hundred feet out, away from all the rocks. A really sleek sixty-something-foot sloop. We asked Lorgan to take us for a sail, but he said he needed his first mate to help, and the dingy to get to the boat was stored a half-mile away and wouldn't take seven people at one time, so we never got to go. It was a beauty, though, even from afar. Strange. I wonder what happened. . . I see the buoy's gone, too, so maybe everything broke loose from the anchor and drifted out to sea during the receding of that high tide that took their bodies with it. Or. . . have there been any big storms around this area lately?"

Nico shook his head pensively. Looking down the hundred-foot drop to jagged rocks that hugged the base of the cliff and poked their sharp edges up here and there from gently rolling waves that lapped against the face of the smooth wall above, he tried to imagine just how high up a high tide would rise over those rocks— And Milo said they were both strong swimmers. . .

"The boat was called 'Dreamer'."

The young men locked eyes with each other.

Milo raised his trumpet and played the last notes of Elyse's upbeat song very slowly, as if it were a requiem, the music from his horn pure and clear and full of sorrow. . .but resonating tenderly into a faint, final tremolo of hope: *This. . .old. . .world. . . is a sweet. . .bal. . .loon*—

Echoes of the trumpet's sounds floated softly out over the sea to be lost in a silent breeze.

OTHER BOOKS BY
ALEXANDRA YORK

CROSSPOINTS A Novel of Choice—English: Promethena Press, world-wide Spanish: Grito Sagrado Press, world-wide Russian: Mir Knigi Press

OVER THE YEARS: Poetry, Lyrics, Songs, Prose—Silver Rose Press

FROM THE FOUNTAINHEAD TO THE FUTURE and Other Essays on Art and Excellence—Silver Rose Press

LOSE 10 YEARS IN 10 DAYS—Hardcover: Macmillan; Paperback: McGraw-Hill

BACK TO BASICS NATURAL BEAUTY HANDBOOK—Hardcover: Van Nostrand and Book-of-the Month Club; Paperback: Berkley-Jove

ALEXANDRA YORK

Alexandra York presently draws from her multi-faceted background to focus on fiction as well as writing and lecturing on the arts and the culture.

In addition to authoring five nonfiction books (one a Book-of-the-Month Club selection), Alexandra has also been published in magazine and newspaper articles, book and movie reviews, and poetry. In other media, she both wrote and performed a bi-weekly feature on WPIX-TV Channel 11 Evening News in New York and wrote and hosted two different Talk Shows that tracked the contemporary performing arts for ABC Radio Network. As an author, she has been a guest on many major Talk Shows, including "The Today Show," "Larry King Live," "To Tell the Truth," "AM New York," "AM Los Angeles," "AM Philadelphia," "Wake-Up Houston," ABC's "Eyewitness News," and hundreds of local and syndicated radio shows. As a performer, she appeared (along with stage and film work) as principal actress in dozens of TV and radio commercials in America and Europe, culminating that aspect of her career in a year-long tour of the U.S. as an exclusive TV spokeswoman for Clairol, Inc. In person, she has lectured extensively at Town Hall Celebrity Series, corporations, universities, and exclusive cruise ships.

Alexandra is published in England, Australia, Mexico, South America, Russia, and Spain, as well as the United States and Canada. Aside from her nonfiction books (Book-of-the-Month Club, Macmillan, McGraw-Hill, Van Nostrand, Ballantine and Berkley-Jove), her work has also appeared in publications as varied as *Reader's Digest* (Domestic and International), *Vital Speeches*, *The New York Times*, *USA Today*, *Vogue*, *New Woman*, *Chronicles*, *The Humanist*, *The Intellectual Activist*, *Reason*, *American Arts Quarterly*, *American Artist* and *Confrontation Literary Journal*. She was for six years the Editor for *ART Ideas*, a quarterly arts and culture magazine published by American Renaissance for the Twenty-first Century (ART) a 501(C)(3) New-York-City-based nonprofit arts foundation of which she is the Founding President: www.ART-21.org

Alexandra received the 1997 Whiting Memorial Award for outstanding service to the cultural world from the International Society for Philosophical Enquiry. She is listed in *Who's Who of American Women* and *Who's Who in America*. With her husband, Barrett Randell, she divides her time between New York City, Bucks County, PA, and Vermont.

www.ingramcontent.com/pod-product-compliance
Lightning Source LLC
Chambersburg PA
CBHW031343170626
46807CB00002B/804